apology

apology

a novel

Jon Pineda

milkweed
editions

The characters and events in this book are fictitious. Any similarity to real persons, living or dead, is coincidental and not intended by the author.

Published 2013 by Milkweed Editions
Printed in the United States of America
Cover design and graphic by Brad Norr
Author photo by Amy Pineda
13 14 15 16 17   5 4 3 2 1
First Edition

Milkweed Editions, an independent nonprofit publisher, gratefully acknowledges sustaining support from the Bush Foundation; the Patrick and Aimee Butler Foundation; the Dougherty Family Foundation; the Driscoll Foundation; the Jerome Foundation; the Lindquist & Vennum Foundation; the McKnight Foundation; the voters of Minnesota through a Minnesota State Arts Board Operating Support grant, thanks to a legislative appropriation from the arts and cultural heritage fund; the National Endowment for the Arts; the Target Foundation; and other generous contributions from foundations, corporations, and individuals. For a full listing of Milkweed Editions supporters, please visit www.milkweed.org.

  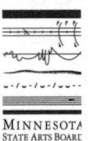   

Library of Congress Cataloging-in-Publication Data

Pineda, Jon, 1971–
    Apology : a novel / Jon Pineda. — 1st ed.
      p.   cm.
    ISBN 978-1-57131-104-7 (acid-free paper)
    I. Title.
    PS3616.I565A85 2013
    813'.6—dc23

                                                    2012027828

Milkweed Editions is committed to ecological stewardship. We strive to align our book production practices with this principle, and to reduce the impact of our operations in the environment. We are a member of the Green Press Initiative, a nonprofit coalition of publishers, manufacturers, and authors working to protect the world's endangered forests and conserve natural resources. *Apology* was printed on acid-free 100% postconsumer-waste paper by Edwards Brothers, Inc.

For Emma and Luke

. . . the sum of these events
I cannot draw, the ledger I cannot keep, the accounting
beyond the account:

—A. R. Ammons, "Corsons Inlet"

apology

one

Tom remembered having to take his red windbreaker. He and his friends had gone to the huge field by the edge of the neighborhood. It was perfect for a game of football. The grass still thick in patches looked like scattered green pillows. You had to climb over a chain-link fence to get there, or else brave the thicket rich with sumac and hornets and slip through a flap that had not been properly secured.

Jumping off the fence, Tom removed his jacket, slinging it. It was tough work climbing. He had broken a good sweat. He also knew his friends. In the game they would have grabbed at the stray hood to rip it from him, use it against him. He didn't want them to have that advantage.

In the distance construction vehicles sat abandoned. Most were monstrous and rigid, rusted. Some yellow as teeth. His friends joked about going over there and seeing if any of those fools who operated them during the day had left the keys in the ignition. They could crank the engines. They could lift the shovel of the excavator, elevate the blunt shield of the bulldozer. "Let's go tear it up," one of them crowed. Another joined in, echoing until it became their chanting. Tom remembered laughing along. He was amazed these kids, most the same age as he was, would feel entitled to do so. Especially when none had dared go that far. Every one of the boys in the neighborhood knew the site was off limits.

Mario, a dumpy kid with a bowl cut, was pointing.

"Hey, *Fino*, isn't that your sister?"

Tom's twin had found the loose panel in the fence. She was standing over by his red windbreaker, which she lifted from the grass and held in her hand. She twirled it into a ball of fire. She called his full name—*Thomas X. Serafino, Thomas X. Serafino!*—and then that it was time for dinner and that he needed to come home. She was already acting like the bossy teacher she wanted to become.

Now his friends were laughing.

"Get out of here, Teagan," he said.

She just stood there and waited for him. She even tapped her foot.

"Get out of my life!" he yelled.

He looked back at his friends, their collective smirk.

The brief disruption in the game gave one of them a chance to take the ball and beam it at anyone who wasn't paying attention. When Tom stared back at Teagan, he took one in the head. The ball wobbled away.

Some of the others scrambled for it. Tom dove, but he wasn't fast enough. Now Mario had it. Tom ran in circles to avoid him, the next hit. They all did. When he looked back at the fence, Tom saw the jacket suspended in air. Teagan had taken one of the sleeves and fished it through the fence's lattice and tied it there like a giant ribbon. But Tom didn't see her. Not at the far corner. Nor beyond the fence to the street leading back into their neighborhood.

He took another one in the head.

As Tom made his way home through the cooling darkness, the game still smeared against his skin, his throat itched with burning. He thought he would find his sister glowering at him, sitting obediently at the kitchen table, but it was his mother, Elinor, who met him at the door.

"Where were you two?" his mother said.

"Just playing ball," he said.

His mother looked past him.

"Is Sissy coming?" she said.

She went to the end of the porch and stared down the street. As if his twin would suddenly appear, as if mere insistence could make it so.

It stayed put. There, in the throat of the pit. The last person to touch it had been a transient the foreman had picked out of a lineup at the local shopping center parking lot. The foreman called the man Shoe. He had come unprepared, with no steel-toed boots to his name.

Rather than sending him away altogether, the foreman ordered the man to the store with a loaned fifty-dollar bill. Shoe walked away from the site, trying not to drag his right foot behind him. When he came back, he could hear the others as he approached. Howling, though they were running their machinery full-on.

The foreman yelled, "*Shoe,* get in there," and threw him a shovel as an afterthought. Earlier, the crew had ripped through a power cable the utility locator missed marking. They were fortunate it wasn't live. The prints indicated hints of buried structure. The foreman didn't want to take any more chances. They would have to hand-dig this section.

It hadn't occurred to the foreman to ask Shoe if he understood. They just needed someone to find the top of the conduit, or, if it was another direct buried cable, then its black plenum sheath. They were already so deep, it couldn't be down much farther, if it was even there at all.

How unnecessary it had been for this young man to slide down the gray clay wall, breaking in the new boots with slick smearing. The foreman pointed at the deepest spot and nudged the air downward, which meant *dig,* and Shoe slipped the shovel head into the already broken muck and began, though there was nowhere to go with it. He didn't know if he could sling it above him and not hit anyone.

They were behind schedule.

It was taking too long.

"Oh, just get the hell out of there," the foreman said to the stooped figure.

Shoe had been this person most of his life. The intended recipient of a cussword, a dredger of malcontent. And now Shoe did not hesitate. He thrust the shovel head in at an angle, prepared to dig more if the man suddenly changed his mind.

The man did not change his mind. Nor did he reach down to help pull Shoe up. It was too slippery, too much sludge for his tasseled loafers. The tool was left there, abandoned in place, and Shoe crawled out, sliding, pulling himself up with all of his might as the few standing around offered him only their ridicule.

That evening, with the sounds of her brother and his friends taunting each other in the nearby field, Teagan walked among the machinery at the construction site. At each vehicle she stopped to inspect the sinuous, exposed hoses connected to what seemed more an open brain than an engine.

There was the unfamiliar smell of diesel. It grafted to her excitement, of having wandered here alone. Cautiously, she stepped between tracks in the matted clay. The tracks now resembled stamped sections of gray Play-Doh, as if the earth had first been rolled out smooth by the workers and then tamped down with metal templates, industrial-sized cookie cutters. The spaced teeth of a backhoe. The track belt fit snug around a bulldozer's wheels. Some fragments of dirt and clay had dried and crumbled at the edges of each one.

Then the machines were a herd of huge animals sleeping.

Near the farthest end of the site, Teagan found a deep hole. At first, it looked like a well. Something from one of the children's books she liked to read. Except there were no walled stones encircling the opening. No small shingled roof with a bucket hanging from coiled rope.

It was already getting late, she knew, but with the vehicles quietly sleeping she could at least peer down into the pit. It would be something to boast about to her twin brother. She was sure neither he nor any of his friends had been brave enough to explore the site alone.

Tommy wasn't the boss of her, she thought, even though she could hear his voice plain as day now, telling her she needed to get out of there—not just his *life*, as he had said it so rudely in front of the others, but *here* as well.

This entire place that was growing darker by the second.

She gulped the cool air and leaned over to take another look.

Her foot began to slip on the edge.

She recovered. She didn't hear bits of falling dirt. No sound of splashing water. She laughed to herself. She was fast, faster than her brother. Yes. It didn't matter that she had almost slipped down into it. She would take precaution and back way up this time, as far back as possible. She would brace her foot against the bulldozer's track as if it were a starting block.

As she readied herself, she felt it, a blow to the head.

"*Owww,*" she yelled and looked around, but saw only a shadow darting out of view. She found the football and held it up. Etched on the side was the name *Mario,* her brother's stupid friend she couldn't stand.

"I have this. It's mine now," she said.

"You wish," came a voice from the other side of the bulldozer.

"*You* wish."

"No, *you* wish."

The voice went back and forth with her this way.

She held the ball with both hands, like she had watched Tommy do countless times as he tore through a bundle of boys on the field, but instead of grunting and making noise in the fray, she stepped slowly, as if replaying a memory of her brother, except that she was her brother now and could turn easily to gain yardage, galloping in slow motion toward the others, who weren't there. She went around one side of the bulldozer and saw him from behind, crouched and hiding. She lifted the ball and threw it at his head.

"Shit," Mario said, throwing a hand up and rubbing behind his ear.

She laughed and ran away as he scrambled for the ball and then took off after her. They wove around the machinery. When they rounded the excavator, Teagan frantically grabbed onto one of the wheels. "Base, Mario!" she yelled. "Base!"

"Nice try, but there's no base," the boy said.

She screamed, frightened and gleeful.

He fired the ball in a perfect spiral. She managed to dodge it. After she was clear of it, she realized she should have grabbed it out of the air and chased after him. She could hear Tommy in her head coaching her, telling her she had just as much right to get it and pelt him good. She didn't know where the ball had gone. She didn't know where the boy had gone either, but she suspected he had the ball again.

There was more tiptoeing around. She wanted to say she was done. All she had wanted to do to begin with was jump across the well and be done with it. That he had stopped her from doing so made her angry, especially now that there had been a slight break in the attack. A reprieve to consider her options. She thought about it and decided she was done with him and even said so, but the boy only laughed, and when he did, she saw that he had somehow climbed up on top of the bulldozer and was looming over her, his arm cocked back.

"You can't jump that pit," he said, pointing in front of them.

"I was about to," she said.

She could hear Tommy telling her to run away.

"There's no way," the boy said. "*I* couldn't even do it."

"So," she said. "That doesn't mean anything to me."

"Then do it," he said.

"I don't feel like it now."

"Because you can't."

"You wish."

"*You* wish."

"I could jump that thing with my eyes closed," she said.

There was a part of her that believed it, too. She had taken ballet on and off over the last few years, when her parents had extra money for the lessons, and she had been told she was a natural. *If only you had started her out sooner,* she remembered hearing the instructor tell her mother.

"You're a joke," the boy said.

He had not brought down his arm, and the ball in silhouette looked for a moment like another head that had grown out of his shoulder. Teagan shuddered.

"Come on then," he said. "We don't have all day."

"For what?" she said.

"Try to jump over it," he said.

She laughed.

"Why are you laughing?" he said.

"Because I know what you're gonna do."

Now the boy was the one laughing. "I won't," he added.

"I know you will. The moment I jump, you're gonna throw it at me."

"I'm telling you I won't."

"Yeah, right."

"Yeah, right nothing."

She looked at him, trying to gauge his expression, but she could see only the faint outline of his face and, beside it, the shadowy second head that had grown more ominous in the evening light.

"Don't be a pussy," he said.

"I'm not a pussy," she said.

"Yes, you are."

She looked at the well and then at him high atop the bulldozer, and she nodded but didn't say anything. She walked nonchalantly back to where she had been to begin with, before he had shown up and hit her with the ball. She placed her shoes against the belt track and leaned forward, placing her fingertips onto the tamped dirt.

She took a breath and held it.

She could feel her heart beating wildly now. Not for this boy or for the dare or for the well itself. She remembered the time she was in ballet class, and the parents had been told they could come into the studio and observe. Against the mirrored walls, the parents sat on the floor with their shoes off, looking oddly out of place, while the young girls stood at one end of the room preparing to run and leap, one by one, over an imaginary puddle on the floor. Teagan had been singled out by the instructor to demonstrate.

She herself wanted to be an instructor one day. A teacher of some sort. But her heart had been tearing through itself at that moment, and she did not dare look at her mother or her father, and definitely not at Tommy. She was fearful of losing any concentration she had.

With all that she could summon, she'd sprinted elegantly as she had been taught and first lifted her right leg straight and pushed with the back left up to where, like a pair of scissors opening, she cut her figure into the air.

She told herself she could do that again.

Not the form so much as the sheer leap itself. She could do it easily, and so without any more thought, she pushed hard and took off toward the well that wasn't a well. It was just a hole in the ground. It would be easy to jump. It would not crumble on the other side where her foot would come down. His laughter chased after her, but she didn't care now. She was going to do it, she knew.

She leapt free, but once in the air, she felt something graze by her. It threw her off. Just briefly. She was too surprised to scream. Her front foot landed at the edge, which then collapsed.

She thought she could hear someone calling her name up above, but it wasn't her name exactly. It was crying that was meant to be her name. Everything smelled wet, and above it, the sound of someone hurt, a sadness falling on top of her.

When she closed her eyes, she could hear it and when she opened her eyes, expecting to hear it again, it ceased, as did the square of the sky, and her head, wet as the smell of wetness, began to warm and then burn. Everything she knew became ashes in her mouth. For the rest of her life she would be able to taste the hint of this day but its memory would have long vanished like a failed fuse.

By the time Shoe made it home to his brother's after work, the others had already eaten and cleaned the dishes and gone about the rest of their night. His nieces were in their bedrooms finishing their homework, and Paul was in the garage trying to fix the edger Mario had taken apart with the intention to reassemble but never did. The boy had only left it a mess.

Shoe carefully set his new boots inside by the front door. They were still caked in mud. There had been plenty of time for the mud to dry on his walk back, but it hadn't. It was his luck. He wished he had his old shoes, but the foreman had thrown them away.

In floppy socks, Shoe scooted into the kitchen, and his frame stooped more so as he looked over the wrapped plates shelved in the fridge. Finding the one that must have been intended for him, he brought it out and did not bother heating it up but sat, instead, at the kitchen table and peeled back the plastic wrapping. He began to spoon the food in quickly. He had forgotten to pack a lunch.

"Exequiel, slow down before you kill yourself," his brother's wife said.

She'd walked in with a basket of clothes fresh from the dryer. He could smell and feel it, their heat. She sat across from him at the table and started folding. As he ate, he looked up every now and then. There were his shirts, his underwear. A stacked tower of his future days before him. He watched her hands smooth the legs of his pants, pulling on the crotch before finishing.

"Aren't you going to ask me how my first day was?" Shoe said.

"If I was your wife, yes," she said.

They sat there for a moment.

He envied Paul's life. Mariposa was a good woman for allowing him into her home. He knew this. As soon as he could save enough for a deposit, he would find a room elsewhere. He would give her back her routine.

"You and Paul should go out one night this week," he said. "I'll watch the kids."

"We could get dressed up and go dancing."

"Yes!" The thought of helping her was exciting.

She looked at him.

"What?" he said.

"You really think I'd leave you alone with my girls?"

The directness of the question shocked him.

"I'm sorry," she said, trying to recover. "That is a nice offer. Thank you."

He looked down at his plate. He had scooped a sizable pit out of the mound of mashed potatoes. The middle was gone. All of the cold gravy he now tasted on the back of his tongue. Mariposa was a good cook, but he would never go so far as to tell her so.

Paul came into the kitchen with his hands raised before him. He was a small man, smaller than Shoe, but more muscular. He looked like a surgeon preparing for a procedure. His forearms were streaked with dark lines of grease that ran down from his hands. The creases in his fingers were just as filthy. Seeing this, Mary jumped up and turned on the hot water in the sink, the entire time scolding her husband for thinking he could clean his hands where she had to wash dishes.

"Where would you have me rinse them, Mariposa?" Paul asked. He was being serious. Shoe snickered and shoveled more mashed potatoes into his mouth. His brother could be funny. For Shoe, it was like watching a show.

"The spigot outside might be one place I'd try," she said.

"You can't loosen it. I need to fix the stem," Paul said. "*Mano,* maybe you could help me with that this weekend?"

Shoe glanced at his brother and nodded.

"Good," Paul said. "See, Mariposa?"

"I see," she said. "But that doesn't mean anything."

Tom sat in his bedroom and put his ear to the wall. He was trying to make out what his father was saying in the other room. Manny Serafino had called the police, and now two officers, greatly staggered in height and looking like odd twins in matching dark-blue uniforms, were sitting in the living room and taking notes. His mother had given them Teagan's school picture from last year. Tom heard one of the officers stupidly say, "Don't worry, Mr. and Mrs. Serafino, we'll find her."

When they left the house, the officers turned on the squad car lights. They didn't turn on the siren, as Tom thought they might have done. Instead, the numbered car drove off quietly in the flashing of colors. The street was suddenly dark, filled only with parked cars belonging to those who lived there.

A few neighbors were standing on their front porches watching the house. Some came over and asked what had happened. Soon after, the husbands left with Tom's father in a caravan of cars.

Tom's mother knocked on his bedroom door and stepped inside to find him shirtless, sitting on the floor beside his dresser, knees bunched up to his chest and body slightly rocking back and forth. He wanted to go back to that moment with Teagan by the fence. He wanted nothing more than to see her twirl the red windbreaker, its transformation into a fireball.

"I shouldn't have told her," he said.

"Told her what, Tommy?" his mother said, taking a seat on the floor next to him.

"It was just so stupid."

"Do you want to tell me?"

Tom shook his head.

"Okay," his mother said.

She was looking around the room, taking it in.

Above his bed was a replica P-51 Mustang he and his father had glued together and painted not long ago. The airplane hung from a single piece of clear fishing line. It gave the appearance of floating in the air.

"I shouldn't have said it."

"What, Tommy? You shouldn't have said *what?*"

There were the signature decals of its razor-like teeth near the propeller. She realized the airplane was slowly turning on its own.

"We were playing football," Tom said. "She kept bugging us."

"Okay," his mother said. She slipped her fingers into his black hair.

"I told her to get out of my life."

He dropped his head and cried.

His mother's hand made its way to his back. She rubbed small circles over his skin.

"You didn't mean it, Tommy," she said.

"But I did," Tom said. "I did mean it."

W hen Shoe woke the next morning, he found himself facedown on the floor. He had fallen off the couch. He had even managed to bring the crocheted throw with him. It had tangled around his legs, as if it were a hammock he had fallen asleep inside, his own little cocoon.

He remembered a time he had jumped a freight train outside of Salinas. He did so thinking he was heading north, and had ended up going east. On one stretch of the trip, oblivious to his misdirection, he had emptied sacks of fruit and used the ripped cloth to make a crude sling. He fastened its ends on the eye hooks that protruded from the rusted metal corners of the storage car. Passing the blistered rows of newly harvested fields, the lines of soil ticking by, Shoe lay in the makeshift hammock and drowsed as best he could.

He checked the digital alarm clock plugged into the outlet by the couch. The clock was something Paul let him use now that Shoe had found a job. It was still early. *Everyone in the family is asleep,* Shoe thought, scratching at his chest and then at the meshy spot on his shoulder. The scar itched. He made an inadvertent noise the way a dog might.

You can't stay here, Exequiel.

The train was years away from him now.

Shoe put on only his pants. His right foot squeaked against the floor. He stopped and changed his walk so that it wouldn't drag, then went into the kitchen to make coffee.

Mary was sitting at the table and reading the morning paper.

Without a shirt on, Shoe felt self-conscious. He tried to suck in his stomach, but it didn't matter. His posture was still slightly broken. As he poured himself a cup, he imagined her staring at the spot on his shoulder that caused him to stoop like a hunchback. It was the wadded flesh of scar tissue that made him look deformed.

He wondered if Paul had ever told her about how they found him that day long ago, when he was still a boy living in another country. Paul had left for the States by then. Paul had not seen the large, fresh wound from which his younger brother had to recover.

"I can make you something," Mary said.

"It's okay."

"No, I don't mind," she said, and set down her paper.

She went to the fridge and took out a carton of eggs and some butter and a bell pepper that had been cut in half and covered with foil. There was also part of an onion she brought out and began to dice. She then cut a pat of butter and slid it onto a warm skillet. When the omelet was finished, she folded it onto a plate and placed it on the table before him. Shoe closed his eyes as if in prayer.

He was trying to memorize her scent.

When he opened his eyes, he saw that she had returned to her chair across from him. As the paper unfolded between them, he noticed her hands gripping the edges lightly. He felt his brother was a lucky man. They sat in silence while he ate.

Shoe wanted to be the first one on site. He kept reminding himself that he had only been sent home the day before, not fired. He still had a chance. He wanted the foreman to pull up in that cream-colored custom Ford truck and see that there was at least one person left in the world who still believed in an honest day's work. He wanted to be standing alongside the boss when the others finally showed up. There would be a sweetness to it.

Shoe even harbored the small hope that the foreman would reconsider the name he had given him; that instead of *Shoe*, perhaps he could be known as *Early Bird* or *Rooster*. He would even settle for some bastardization of Exequiel. *X*, or *Zeke*.

But after some thought, really, what did he care?

When he reached the site, Shoe went behind the portable urinal and relieved himself. A breeze sent a shock of cool air between his legs. His scrotum recoiled from the chill. There in the thicket of milkweed and other random brush, he stood listening to his piss hiss against the fiberglass siding.

He considered for a moment climbing up on the bulldozer to cover the driver's seat. The white guy who had operated it yesterday had been a real cocksucker to him, laughing and yucking it up the loudest. But when Shoe finished, his mind leapt to sitting at the table with Mary. He found that despite this environment of strange machinery and torn earth, he could easily recall the memory of her scent. The implication of tenderness.

It was strange to be standing there and thinking of his brother's wife in this way. He did not want his brother's wife, it was not that. His life seemed to him a series of moments in which he felt adrift, felt both the ease and unease of being temporarily settled, then uprooted, felt the odd comfort that was in such an existence. And if he did not necessarily feel adrift, then perhaps he felt something entirely opposite. Perhaps he sensed a permanence around which the rest of his life revolved endlessly.

Shoe could sense his own future complacence. It scared him.

He glanced around. There was the calmness of the bulldozer and the excavator. There were the tracks in the dirt and scattered sand. The evenness of the machine and the tread of his own boots. Down the road there were headlights of vehicles leaving the driveways of the neighborhood, but not one was headed this way.

He was not thinking of his brother's wife now. He was not wishing that it was her hands on him. It was someone else he remembered. A shadowy wall and her silhouette alongside it, sliding down onto her knees. She wanted to take him and hide him inside her. Her mouth was a lovely prison, he felt. He could spend his life there.

Her memory neared him, the smooth edges falling away. He could not get inside her fast enough. Before he could settle on the image, before he could see her entirely again, he immediately felt ashamed and crouched, rubbing his palm over the streaked wall and then to the grass and dirt.

All of it was cold already, its dampness. He imagined Mary coming now with a basket of warm clothes; her folding, and then handing him one of his own clean T-shirts to use.

Shoe, in his stooped way, walked around to the other side of the urinal. He dragged his right foot behind him. The boot made walking more difficult. Shoe put his lunchbox on top of a sawhorse and leaned against the equipment, waiting for anyone to appear at that point.

Where were they? Where were those who had ridiculed him for trying to pull himself out of the mess of the pit? They were probably at home still, rummaging in the darkness of their rooms while their wives slept off sickly sweet hangovers, or the crackling emptiness of meth.

Or there were no wives and never had been. He knew this situation best.

And what hadn't he tried in the years it had taken him to arrive at this one moment? There were nights fused with white light burning, weeks lost entirely to his compulsions. Each time, it was mostly the same. Everything, in one form or another, left him hollowed out and waiting, or searching, for something to inhabit that space.

Once, when he had finished up a job in North Carolina, he left the empty motel where he was staying and walked across a nearby field. It was dusk, and he had come upon a design of poles that resembled a ship's masts, the hull of that ship run aground in the surrounding farmland.

Hanging from the horizontal tiers were gourds painted white. Wide symmetrical holes had been bored into the bulbous ends. Martins were falling out of the sky, darting into the numerous shells of homes someone had taken the time to make for these birds. The gourds swung like pendulums, though at stranger intervals. Shoe had given up on chemicals by then. This image had come too late to warn him away from the life he had already led.

As for women, those he had loved were faceless, despite his attempts at summoning their images. Or they had merged into the same woman.

He couldn't remember which. Sometimes the culmination of memories made her hideous. Or if a passing thought came into sharp enough focus for him to give it his attention, she was always almost pretty. He could make out the outline of her eyes, or just fragments of the collective eyes that stared back at him from his past. Sometimes he laughed at his egalitarian lust. The shapes their eyes became, the different colors that made shadows, or the thick, salty scent of their skin, waves of hair that crashed endlessly within his mouth.

There had been one woman actually.

He had met her in a bar in Taos. He had taught the woman's son to play chess, and sometimes, if it was still light when he came home from work, he and the boy would go out in the yard and kick a ball around.

He felt terrible when the boy, after some months, called him Dad. The mother had encouraged it. He could think of sadder things, yes, and it felt good to be someone's father. Even if he knew he could never be the kind of man who would welcome the responsibility for the remainder of his life.

This mother and her son didn't think it would be temporary.

It was this thought that haunted him some mornings when he woke, reaching absentmindedly for the emptiness beside him, or cocking his ear toward the ghost room that held the memory of the child, that same child waking in the dark and crying for him—*Dad! Dad!*—and him waking, hearing the call, and dragging his body into the darkness to disappear.

Shoe ran a hand along the nicked wood of the sawhorse; a determined hit to the largest cut could snap the sawhorse in half. He laughed at the thought. He knew he was no Bruce Lee.

If he owned a watch, he would have checked his wrist. He started to wonder if he had made a mistake. Had he missed the foreman telling the rest of the crew that they would have the day off? This seemed an impossibility. It wasn't the weekend. *But still,* Shoe thought.

He struggled to climb on top of the bulldozer. Once there, he looked beyond the nearest street and out to the main road that fed into the neighborhood. There were headlights coming this way now, and he was glad for it. He decided it would probably be a good idea to have his shovel by his side once the foreman pulled up.

Still hunched over, with his right shoulder weighing him down as usual, he walked as best he could to the pit and turned around, easing his way into it. Like he was guiding himself down a ladder, rung by rung. His boots slid into the moist clay. Nothing seemed to have dried since he was last in this space.

When he reached the bottom, he stumbled. Something was on the ground. It made him fall against the far wall. When he looked down by his boots, there was just enough light to see the girl slumped on the floor, her head next to the shovel. Everything was still.

Shoe yelled, but his voice didn't reach above him. He panicked. He tried to climb out with one huge jump, gripping near the opening, but he slid back down as if in slow motion. He tried again. Still, he fell back.

He thought she was dead.

The gash along the side of her head looked suddenly severe, as did the swathe of matted hair. Light was beginning to fill the space between them. Dark blood, he could see now, was what coated her hair and the side of her face. Shoe fell to his knees. He put his ear to her nose and mouth.

Why didn't you do this sooner?

He didn't mean to move her head, but he did. Now there was a tiny flutter of breath that kept returning.

He started to cry.

He knew she was alive.

A ball with his nephew's name lay beside her.

For some reason, he picked it up and threw it out of the pit as hard as he could. Then he pulled the shovel out of the ground. The blade made a small sucking sound. He chucked it free of the pit.

His only thought now was that he needed to get her out, but there was no way he could do it alone. He wiped his face and took a deep breath. What had made him think that things had changed, or even that they were going to change?

Above was the world that would not believe him. Above was the world that would not think it was possible that he of all people would have shown up to work early. Nor that he had simply found this girl unconscious, fallen down into the pit where he had been the day before.

He could not summon any logic.

Nothing made sense, except for what he already knew of certain things. When had anything ever gone in his favor? Long ago he had jumped a train, expecting to see more of northern California, maybe even parts of Oregon, and instead, the farmlands outside the freight car's sliding door eventually ended with sign after bewildering sign for elsewhere. His intentions occupied one space while his body occupied another.

He could not bring himself to look at her again. There was more light now.

The girl's cough startled him.

Her eyes were open; the pupils of each were dark as her hair.

He looked away. He closed his eyes.

Above him were the holes in the painted gourds. Large holes that were doorways into the same structured hollowness. An inexplicable nothingness that he had, from time to time, mined with a bent spoon and a tiny flame.

"I'll call someone," he pleaded as he tried to climb out of the pit. "I'll make sure they know you're here. I won't forget you."

He picked up the shovel. He thought of ridiculous things like the prints made by the tread of his boots. Should he go back down and try to smear them clean? Would that even be possible? All was evidence that someone as insignificant as himself had actually existed. This thought was a tormenting one.

But there were very few things that tied him to this world after all. His brother and his family, yes. The few bleary Polaroids stashed in a drawer somewhere in Taos, he imagined. He would wipe the shovel down and drop it in a nearby ditch. The murk of water would clean the rest. He didn't want to be spotted carrying it any farther than he had to.

He dragged his foot behind him as he tried to leave the site. He felt he was being pulled down. Tackled from behind. That's when he remembered the football, his nephew's name on it. It seemed important to remove that from the site too. He didn't know why or what it meant. He searched the brush near the pit. He couldn't find it.

Then he did.

The ball lay hidden in the grass like some kind of giant egg. He picked it up, as if he were being watched, and slipped the ball under his flannel shirt. He hunched to hide this held object. Pressed to his side, it felt like a tumor that had moved on its own, out of his body and into a strange kind of freedom that was never meant to be.

No, it was a stolen egg from long ago.

Shoe made one phone call, an anonymous one to the company office. The receptionist was a silver-haired woman named Josie, whose large collection of Hummel figurines from home had eventually found their way to her desk at work. She was busily arranging them into a kind of narrative when the phone rang. The interruption flustered her slightly at first, and then the cord almost tipped her cup of coffee. It was all she could manage not to yell into the phone as she put the receiver to her ear.

Shoe cupped the bottom half of the phone with his hand. His nieces were in the next room arguing with each other over whose turn it was with the hair dryer. They were getting ready for school. He wished he had chosen a quieter space, or even better yet, had called from a pay phone. *That would have been the smart thing to do,* he could hear his childhood friend Vin goading him.

"Excuse me, sir, but I kent hur you," Josie had calmed down but was fumbling over her own accent. She reached for the small boy in a kelly-green short coat and orange bow tie. He had his eyes closed and was singing his song into the air above him. It didn't make sense to have him facing the statue of a woman carrying a basket of flowers in one hand and holding a little girl's hand in the other. The woman wasn't the girl's mother anyway. The woman was taking the girl to her mother.

"There's been an accident," Shoe said.

"A *what,* honey?" Josie said. She decided on putting the boy to the farthest end, where he could sing out over the edge of the desk. Past the clear plastic square of paper clips and out into the void of the office. Then Josie put on the glasses hanging from a thin chain around her neck and glanced at the clock on the far wall and wrote the time on a pink pad where she normally recorded Mr. Towson's *While You Were Out* messages.

"Go on," Josie said into the phone.

It sounded to Shoe like the woman had said *gone.*

"Go on," Josie said again, slower from her irritation.

"At the site near Pinewood Meadows," Shoe said, trying to picture the billboard nearest the entrance that zigzagged until it reached the huge field, where the giant machinery was. "You'll find a girl there. She's hurt."

"What girl?" Josie said, writing down *Pinewood Meadows.*

Then her wide eyes fell right to the little girl on her desk. This one wore a bonnet that matched the half-oval lace apron tied around her green and orange dress. She was being led home to her mother. Josie studied the figurine, the painted commas of the girl's gleeful eyes. The flower basket woman's matching happiness. Maybe they could hear the boy singing after all. Maybe the boy's voice was so bad that it had brought them joy.

In the hours before dawn he woke, having heard a noise in the kitchen. It was too early for it to be Mary. He felt around in the dark. There was nothing for him to use as a weapon. Over near the front door, he bent down and felt around blindly. One of his new boots fell against his arm. He decided, at the very least, he could swing it so that the hard end, the hidden steel, would strike first. That would knock someone unconscious.

He rounded a corner into the small dining room. There was the sound of glass clinking against glass. When he could see into the kitchen, he found the refrigerator light cast across his nephew's face. The boy looked surprised to see his uncle staring at him. He nearly dropped the gallon of milk he was holding with both hands.

"Sorry, *Tio*," Mario said. "I missed dinner."

"Where were you?"

Mario drank from the milk carton and put it back in the refrigerator. He closed the door so he didn't have to see the scar on his uncle's shoulder. The only light in the kitchen was coming in as a faint, yellow glow from the bulb over the neighbor's garage door. It was enough to frame his uncle's silhouette.

Mario took a seat at the table by the window. He opened the curtain so that more light could come in. Shoe, seeing his nephew do this, dragged himself over to a seat and sat opposite the boy. Shoe waited for him to speak.

Outside, there were the sirens of emergency vehicles. Their blaring so far away. The sound wasn't entirely unpleasant. Shoe's eyes had adjusted, and he could see his nephew making a fist with one hand and covering it with the next. Then the boy traded off, so that the hand that had been a covering was now a fist; the prior fist, a covering.

"You brought back my football," Mario said.

"I found it," Shoe said.

"Where?"

"Where do you think?"

Mario bit his bottom lip, pulling it down against his tongue.

"Were you there?" Shoe said.

He wanted his nephew to deny it. He wanted the boy to wonder aloud that he had loaned it to the girl, or to another boy even. That he didn't know where his football had been. That way Shoe would know for sure.

Mario made a fist with the other hand and covered it again.

Shoe remembered when he had been Mario's age, before he had been taken by the old man and his soldiers. Paul was pulling him aside and asking why he had stolen eggs from the neighboring houses. When Shoe had denied any wrongdoing, Paul had hit him so hard across the head that Shoe thought he was going to throw up. He didn't know how to tell his older brother that it had been a joke, that the other boys were testing him and he was going to go through with it, even though he didn't like eggs back then. It was supposed to make his friends laugh.

They could hold these things in their hands, these little stones the color of snow, not that any of them had ever seen snow; but the deal was that Shoe, the boy Exequiel, was to take as many as he could find and hide them until each rotted and became splotchy gray and shadowy. He and his friends were going to use them as weapons against one another. The smell would stay on whomever had been struck. It would be funny to see the adults crinkle their noses as the targeted boy passed them in the square, everyone wondering then what terrible thing had died.

"So you know?" Mario said.

Shoe nodded, but he wasn't sure if his nephew saw him do so. "Yes," he said.

Mario heaved, trying to hold in his breath, but he couldn't. It blurted out, like air suddenly escaping a balloon. He thought she would have gone home on her own, but today, Tom wasn't at school and then he heard that she had been found and was now in a hospital. He could cry remembering her leaping in the air and him, stupid as he was, thinking only of beaming her good with the ball.

"What happened?" Shoe said.

"We were just playing," Mario said. "I was chasing her. We were throwing the ball at each other. I threw it at her and she fell. I thought she was kidding. It was so dumb, Tio. Anyone could have made that jump!"

"You threw the ball at her?"

"I was playing."

"That's how she fell?"

His uncle's last question made him cry.

"I know it was stupid," Mario said.

He bunched both fists and covered his eyes with them.

The yellowing light brushed his nephew. Shoe leaned across the table to pull one of the fists down, but Mario drew back and continued to hide his face. He coughed against his folded arms.

When Paul had hit Shoe for stealing, Paul had been the one to weep immediately. Somewhere along the line his brother Exequiel had strayed. Of the lessons their parents had taught them both, Paul had been the only one who took them to heart.

Shoe watched his nephew. He thought for a moment that he was seeing his brother Paul again, that he himself had been the one to throw the ball at the girl and that the girl had fallen right before his eyes. This boy, a younger version of Paul, had just reprimanded him for stealing away some part of this girl's life, and yet, at the same time, Shoe saw himself in this same boy as well. The boy's presence was like a door opening onto every version of himself, every boy he had ever known.

"Why didn't you tell anyone?" Shoe said finally.

"I wanted to, but I was scared. I thought they would think I tried to hurt her."

"But you did by not telling anyone."

"Yes," Mario said, bringing his arms down now. "But not like that. I wasn't trying to *hurt* her. It was just a game."

"I know," Shoe said, leaning back. Part of the chair felt cold against his skin. It made him almost shiver. Hearing his nephew's words—*It was just a game*—caused him to pause. He swallowed. As if he could take back the words. Not that he had uttered them, but he would take them in, maybe hide them behind his scar.

"What should we do, Tio?" Mario said.

The question lay on the table between them.

He realized then he should have just left things in place. He should have climbed out of the pit and run as best he could with his foot as it was and found a phone, any phone, and called an ambulance directly. He wanted to go back in time and make a different choice.

Or go back even further.

Back to a time when he was still a boy in another country. There were no hard questions, no actions to take other than waking and surviving and laughing in between those moments. He could barely see his nephew's face. He knew his presence in this boy's life had compromised the situation.

Worse, still, was having left the child. Not that he could have saved her himself, but he could have been the one to save her. Maybe his life could be different if only he had a way to get back to certain moments. He could still hear a boy from another life saying, *Check,* and then laughter when Shoe looked bewildered at the chessboard.

It was the foreman, Mr. Towson, whose picture was in the paper the next day. His white comb-over and large square teeth. His dark eyes. He had been the one to find the girl. He did not mention the anonymous call to the office. He did not mention Josie to the reporters. He was being hailed as a hero.

Mary had come into the kitchen and pointedly set the paper down so that the article was faceup, like the girl had been.

"They didn't know your name, did they?" she said.

"No," Shoe said.

She nodded.

"There's no way for them to know?"

"I don't think so. I never filled out any paperwork."

When he had come back the morning before, only an hour or so after leaving for work, she did not question him. He wasn't her husband. He could do what he pleased. Only that night did she find out from Paul that his brother had quit his new job. Not only that, but Shoe would be leaving for another job opportunity farther south. Now there was this, and her heart felt heavy.

Mary scanned the article.

"Paul is going to see this," she said. "He'll recognize the company name."

"I know it."

"You've brought us bad luck."

Shoe did not have an answer.

"You know that, don't you?" she said.

"Yes."

"We've worked too hard to make a life for our family."

"I know," he said.

"You don't know."

He wished she would make him breakfast now, as she had done the morning before. But that was over. He knew it. He would spend the rest of his life, wherever he happened to be, thinking about those hands of hers.

two

The pediatric ward had been decorated with an undersea theme. Tom followed behind his father as they wove through a corridor full of young children in wheelchairs, some pushing themselves and others being pushed by their parents or by nurses with round, pleasant faces.

Someone had taped a laminated sketch of a blue octopus with orange polka dots over the water fountain. Its suckered arms curved, undulating toward the floor. Tom was thirsty, but he wasn't going to ask his father to stop. He knew his sister had come to, and it was exciting.

He wanted to ask her if she remembered anything.

He especially wanted to tell her he was sorry for what had happened, for telling her to get out of his life. He hadn't wanted that at all and he was prepared to play whatever game she wanted to play now. He would go wherever it was she wanted him to go.

"You need to move your legs," his father said to him.

They passed more children in wheelchairs. Tom found himself nodding at each one, smiling. He hoped they understood he wasn't making fun. He was letting them know in his own way he had yet to see his sister.

From the ceiling hung ornaments of starfish suspended at various lengths by clear fishing line, just like his model airplane. The starfish twirled as he and his father walked past in a rush. They could have been snowflakes from a distance.

At the end of the corridor, his father knocked on a wide door and then pushed it open slowly. They walked inside to find his mother sitting beside the bed. Teagan was sitting up, looking confused. His mother was feeding her red wobbly squares of JELL-O.

"They used to call that *nervous pudding*," his father said, wringing his hands. "I read that in a history book once."

"Who did?" his mother said.

She kept feeding Teagan.

His sister sloppily licked at her lips.

"Hey, Sissy," Tom said.

Teagan's head drooped in a curve, as if on a swivel, but then lifted back up temporarily. It repeated its track. She grinned on its upswing and red liquid dripped down her chin. Across the side of her head was a gash that had been clamped shut with sutures. He could see the chewed condition of her hands, her fingertips busted along the nail beds.

"You *silly goose*," his mother said and wiped his sister's mouth.

"What's wrong with her?" Tom said.

He didn't care that Teagan had to hear him ask it.

His father looked right at him and then pointed him out into the hallway. The place they had rushed to reach, Tom was now being told to leave.

The door closed heavily behind him.

Tom stood next to a fire extinguisher mounted on the wall.

Someone had decorated his sister's door with a laminated drawing of a giant seahorse. He had not noticed it on his way in. Purple and pink, it had huge, cartoonish eyes. The length of the seahorse's body curled like a question mark. It was something Teagan would have loved to have drawn herself, he thought. If she still could do such things.

For those first weeks, Mario would not ride his bike anywhere near Tom's house. He didn't want to make eye contact with Tom, for fear of what he might say should he glimpse his friend's grief. He didn't want to see Teagan again, not that he would anytime soon. She was still recovering in the hospital; but just the thought of her remembering him in that moment made him sick. He prayed she would forget.

Each day he pictured looking into her eyes and seeing some smaller version of himself looking back, staring down as he had from the top of the pit. Stories on the investigation had taken over the local paper, and there was coverage on all of the news channels. The exact details on the progress of the investigation were being withheld by the authorities. All that was revealed was that someone had come forward and mentioned having seen a man that morning in the general vicinity. For a time, children weren't allowed to go outside at all. Parents were fearful this person might be out to harm other children. A neighborhood task force had been assembled. Even Mario's father had joined.

At first the person everyone was looking for was a black man in his early to late thirties, medium build, with a Yankees ball cap. While that was the description being broadcast, Mario felt he could breathe easier. Sometimes he wished he had gone to Tom and told him everything. It was not too late.

He thought, at the very least, he could come forward and say he had seen someone else, but then he knew questions would follow, and they would ask him to describe this person, and he imagined himself sitting in front of a police officer and having to conjure a face that did not exist. That would have been worse, to have sent them on a wild goose chase. He decided he was doing the right thing by saying nothing.

But then another person came forward.

A woman, before beginning her breakfast shift, had dropped off her infant daughter at daycare. The daycare center was at an intersection near the service road entrance to the Pinewood Meadows site. When she was leaving there, the woman had seen a man coming down the road.

He was carrying a shovel, which didn't strike her as odd, but it was the way he carried himself. He was dragging his foot behind him. Lurching. She thought he might be having a heart attack. He was tugging at his shirt, then bending over, trying to steady himself with the shovel. She did not drive off just then. Instead, the woman kept watching him, to see if he was all right. If she explained it correctly, her boss would understand.

She turned her car and drove toward the man. He stumbled in the direction of a newly constructed drainage ditch. Before he vanished into its surrounding brush, she saw his face clearly. The look was of one about to slip entirely underwater, but willingly so. There was no hint of panic in his eyes. His movements were almost graceful.

She didn't dare stop the car. As she continued on, she felt foolish for having thought she could have been of any help. She could hear her ex-boyfriend, as if he were sitting beside her in the passenger seat, his painfully pointy cowboy boots on the dashboard.

"What the fuck kind of thing is *that* to do?" he would have said.

She could see him sneering at her intent. Laughing even, remarking the guy was just looking for a place to piss in peace.

The very next day, after she had seen the man disappear, she took her daughter on a road trip to her sister's, a few hours south in Raleigh. Not that her ex was still calling the house, but she needed time away. She had saved up money. It would allow her a nearly two-week break from having to come home each evening smelling of sausage and coffee.

And rarely had there been time to spend with her daughter outside of the usual schedule; by the time the two made it home, it was dinner for the daughter, then a bath, and then maybe a small block of quiet when they both would lie on the bed and the little girl would grab at the footies of her pajamas and rock back and forth and blow wet raspberries in the shared air between them.

The time with her sister had been welcome. The woman managed to catch up on sleep, which she hadn't realized she needed until she got large doses of it, her sister waking to tend to the daughter, and the woman breathing a sigh of relief into the pillow.

When she finally came back into town, the woman found the rest of the waitstaff at the restaurant talking about the manhunt that had been going on since she had left. No arrests had been made, they said. Her boss mentioned the description of the person the police were hoping to find.

That night, with her daughter on the bed, smiling, the wet gurgling of the child's laughter warding off the drudgery of the day, the woman talked to her daughter and told her the wanted person was not a black man. She went on to describe the shovel he'd held and the strange way he'd walked. The little girl cooed, and the woman nodded.

"Yes, that's right," she said. "He wasn't wearing a baseball cap, and he wasn't black, and he had a nose that looked like this . . ." She made a honking sound as she playfully squeezed her daughter's nose.

The little girl squealed.

I have seen him, the woman thought, and I could set this thing straight. She knew her ex would talk her out of it, and because of that, she was glad he was gone. Besides, how often were there chances to make things right in this world?

Tom went outside to get the paper for his father. His father could not start his day now without trying to finish the paper's crossword puzzle. He would roll it up and carry it with him to the naval operations base, where he would keep it on his desk and glance at it every now and then.

If he had to go to the piers and inspect one of the ships, he would bring the crossword puzzle with him. The air would be laced with diesel and other noxious fumes, and he would care only for the answer that would allow him to fill in blocks going either up and down or side to side. He checked off the inventory of one delivery in supply, and then had a sailor, newly assigned, drive him to the next destination along the bustling piers while he reassessed the answers to the puzzle so far, thinking perhaps he had chosen wrong letters, which would have sent him guessing in the wrong direction. Sometimes he asked the sailor driving, who was usually a kid from the Midwest. More often than not, the sailor wouldn't have a clue.

Tom usually didn't care for the news, but with the manhunt on, he found he wanted to scan the front page of every paper, in hopes of being the first to learn of an arrest. An arrest had the power to change everything. He had been scared, had not been able to go out and play with friends these last weeks, and at school, the other kids wouldn't talk to him. As if doing so, he thought, would make them a target like Teagan.

When Tom unfolded the morning paper, he found the revised rendering. It was a sketch of an entirely different man. Tom couldn't believe it. He looked at the face and laughed uncontrollably for a few seconds, all while confusion swirled in his head. Then he felt sick. It was him. Tom knew it. He ran into the house so the others would know it too.

It had been at least a year since they had tried assembling another model.

"I thought you wanted to put this together?" his father said.

Tom folded the directions and placed them on top of the small cardboard box. Sheets of gray plastic parts rattled inside like pieces in a board game. Normally, he would have gone straight for the colorful decals. Red, white, and blue emblems. Elaborate insignias. Now he just wanted to see the plan written out in English, alongside the other languages. Within this collection of words was a sequence they could use.

"Do I have to talk to myself today?" his father said.

Tom smirked.

"Where did Mom take Sissy?"

"Don't worry about it. It's just for the day."

His father rummaged through the bag from the hobby store and pulled out a fresh metal tube of Testors glue.

"To that new place?" Tom said.

His father liked to use a *balisong*. The butterfly knife. He spun the handle until it split open. His hand blurred as the blade emerged within the practiced twirl. Once he locked the handle at the end, he used the blade to slice each plastic piece free. He started with the largest parts, the halved fuselage, the wings, working his way down to the wheels of the functionless landing gear.

"Don't you want to do this? I thought you wanted to do this?"

Tom shrugged. He focused on the tiny bottles of paint his father was lining up in a spectrum, from dark to light colors.

"We're missing yellow for this part here."

Tom touched the picture on the side of the box. The artist's rendition of the WWII bomber had it floating among a wisp of clouds.

"We don't have to use the same color just because they did," his father said.

"Oh," Tom said.

Tom looked down at his hands. They were open, with the palms facing up, resting in his lap. He counted his fingers. In a few days, he would be eleven. So would Teagan.

Behind them on the refrigerator was a drawing. It was covered in creases that had been smoothed over. Teagan had made it in school earlier that day, the night she had gone missing.

After the police had shown up and his father had left with others in search of her, the house was eventually held in the steady breathing of his mother and the few who had come to hold vigil. Tom, unable to sleep, had crept into the kitchen, where he grabbed the drawing, scooting away the refrigerator magnets, and carried it back to bed, where he slept with it.

In the morning, it, too, had disappeared. Frantic, he tore through his covers. He eventually found it mashed at the bottom of the bed. It would be years before he would picture the way he must have kicked at it in his sleep, how he must have secretly wanted it gone for good.

The bomber took them most of the day to finish because his father decided they should try to make it as close to the real thing as possible. The switch confused Tom.

"You know, that's what's important, Tommy."

Tom didn't remind him their model would look different from the one in the picture.

When his father left the room, Tom touched a bright ring of color near one of the engines. It was just to see if it had dried all the way. His fingertip caught briefly in the tack. He stared at the spot, his fresh red print. Lines ran parallel and others converged.

He remembered one of the courtroom exhibits, the photograph of the ball, blown up to show the blotted dots of his sister's blood. Mario's uncle had sat quietly while the easel was adjusted and the photograph on foamboard was replaced with another, the next one displaying the shovel's blade alongside the zipper-like gash on Teagan's shorn head.

One of the lawyers brought out the actual shovel, which had been wrapped in heavy translucent plastic and taped at each end. The woman, dressed in a dark-gray business suit, grabbed the long handle just under the head and held it out to the jury. Tom remembered she had simply asked, "Can you even imagine?"

She raised the weapon high.

It was as if a string had been connected from the end of the blade to the eyelids of those jury members, for their eyes grew wide as the raised shovel approached them, their necks cast back in dramatic choreography.

Tom had started talking under his breath. It was uncontrollable.

Mario's uncle had not moved once, his head fastened in place so that his gaze fell squarely on the judge in front of him, a man whose own face was comprised mostly of large, whitish eyebrows and a matching mustache.

Shoe had seen this man before. Not this particular man, but one who inhabited a similar space in his life. Hadn't he felt the identical eyes of judgment long before now? He watched the bristling expression, the black velvet robe mirroring the shadows of a lost country. Its memory threatened to envelop the man's face altogether.

He would let the chaos come in the form it would take. As it always did. And what was that voice, barely audible now, a boy speaking behind him, trying to get his attention, whispering, "I hope you . . . ," and then so clearly now, "die . . . I hope you die!" That voice seemed to be the one living inside his head as the woman lawyer, out of the corner of his eye, kept swinging the shovel skyward, as if she were the only one trying to escape this pit where the floor, made now of sand and then wholly of light, fell as soon as it formed.

Nights, Tom lay in bed and glanced over at the B-52 that was forever grounded on his dresser. He *could* imagine, as the lawyer had posed the question that day, but when he did now, parts of his life pulled away. Were swept up and scattered. He thought hard for Teagan, too.

The future had become a distant, unattainable target.

Sometimes he would hear her down the hall. From her room, she would be yelling and, if she was especially upset, beating one of her dolls against the wall.

In the morning, at breakfast, he would find her at the table crying over the doll's broken face. Inevitably, their father would come home later in the evening with a wrapped present, and she would never be able to guess what was inside. Until the paper was finally torn back and her face grew bright, full of such honest surprise, it made Tom catch his breath.

Her one wish was to see the geese and so they went to Mount Trashmore in Virginia Beach. At one of the picnic tables by the lake, their mother strewed twisted pink and blue rolls of crepe paper, frozen in waves. It was just them.

After a while, Teagan tore off some of the decorations and fashioned the pieces into a headband. She danced around the table while she helped her mother finish setting up. Manny had gone to the top of the hill and was looking past the picnic area to the fleet of paddleboats dotting the man-made lake.

Tom took a seat beside him, breathing heavily.

"Are you an old man now?" Manny said, smiling.

"Not as old as you," Tom said.

"That's true. It took me much longer to get here."

He laughed to himself.

"Gross, what's that stuff there?" Tom said.

"Where?"

"Those spots along the side."

He pointed to the rivulets of rust-colored liquid oozing from the ground.

"Trash," Manny said. "Loads of it right under us."

Tom tried to imagine the accumulation of other people's things. Diapers. Baseball gloves. Crushed globes.

"It's disgusting." He shook his head.

"It has to go somewhere, Tommy," his father said.

They both regarded the lake. People were pedaling the little boats across the white surface. Tom wanted his father to say something, but Manny was already thinking about another time, a life long before this one.

. . . .

"Did you know we used to play a game about you?" Tom offered.

"Who?"

"Me and Teagan."

"What game? What was this game?"

"When you were out to sea . . ."

"You were too young to remember those times."

"That's not true. We'd play BATTLESHIP. Except we changed the rules. We had to choose a piece and say that's where you were. You were inside that little boat. We'd put it back on the board and both of us would start praying out loud."

Manny smiled.

"You wanted to sink it, yes, Tommy? You wanted to drown *dear old Dad*."

"No," Tom said, shaking his head. He was suddenly serious. "The object was to miss it."

"Miss?"

"That way you'd stay alive."

Manny didn't look at his son. He watched Teagan chasing one of the speckled geese that had wandered over near the picnic area. She was flapping her arms like she had become one of them, like she could take flight at any moment.

Elinor had found a place about an hour and a half drive from Norfolk. It had a reputation for being one of the best rehabilitation centers in the state. Manny liked the idea of Teagan receiving specialized care, but the location meant she would have to stay at the facility throughout the week. He wasn't ready for that just yet.

This thought of separation had become increasingly difficult, and yet imagining it sometimes filled him with such relief he was immediately stricken with guilt. Elinor did not understand it. She said he of all people had no right to be so protective, let alone feel guilty. His naval deployments had left a *huge hole* in their family life, she had said once. He had never forgotten it.

At one of the centers they had visited, there had been a girl. He had seen her sitting alone in the cafeteria. Elinor and the kids were exploring the courtyard. He spotted them through the main facility windows, Teagan holding out her arms straight now and pretending to be an airplane. Tom stood around with his hands in his pockets.

The girl in the cafeteria slumped forward in her wheelchair, and Manny noticed, as he neared her, that she was mestiza. A part of him felt it was his duty to stop and talk to her, even though he didn't know if she could speak, let alone understand him.

"How are you today?" he said.

The girl in the wheelchair looked up at him.

One of her eyes had a blown pupil. He had seen this before, back when he was a child in the islands, walking through the marketplace with his *lola*. There had been a man selling an assortment of fish. Beside the man had been a boy holding a cigar box filled with coins, looking oddly like the parent, with an authoritative smirk. The man's face had fallen on one side, the eye, nearly black in its entirety, trying to hold it up.

The girl in the wheelchair could have been Manny's daughter.

Manny shook his head. She was someone's daughter.

Or had been.

"Was your lunch good?" he said to the girl.

She smiled at him with her broken face. She raised her hand and moved her fingers in the air. She waited for him to respond.

For a moment, he was a boy again and whatever had made this girl who she was to become had yet to occur. He could hear his lola telling him not to stare. The sound of her voice came to him from a great distance, across a ghost ocean, and now he waded out into it.

*A*t first, I thought you were my dad. You kind of look like him. He comes to visit when he can, but he lives so far away, you understand.

The janitor tells me it's okay. The janitor is nice. He cleans the floors and fixes things. I hear some of the nurses talk about him, but I don't care. I think they're just jealous because he checks on me.

Sometimes he's like an older brother, but lately, he's been telling me that I'm his girlfriend now. That when I get old enough, he's going to marry me and take me away from this place. I tell him, "Yeah right, Buster." He doesn't understand me, doesn't understand sign language.

No one here seems to understand.

three

They had gathered in the old football stadium. Tom was already sitting quietly with other boys from his grade. Mr. Rochambeau, the vice principal of their junior high, was busy berating the students who had yet to settle. Most of them, a mix of the school's seventh, eighth, and ninth graders, raced up and down the wide metal bleachers.

Mr. Rochambeau's plaintive voice vanished into the afternoon air. No one seemed to be listening. His voice grew higher in pitch, forcing a clip of feedback on the already stressed PA system. Tom ducked his head and mimicked the man's slight lisp. He had studied this trait to some degree these last few years, and was known in certain circles for doing a pretty decent impersonation.

Tom's friends nodded in approval.

"Good one, *Fino*," they all said.

Normally a tall, stooping figure in the school's hallways, Mr. Rochambeau looked tiny, his stature diminished where he stood next to a podium someone had placed directly on the fifty-yard line. "People, please," Mr. Rochambeau pleaded into the microphone. His voice echoed briefly over the field.

"*Pweeple*," Tom mimicked.

Tom's friends laughed.

"All right, all right," Mr. Rochambeau continued. "The sooner we settle down, the sooner we can sign these yearbooks. And go about our lives."

Some kids who were running the bleachers paused at the resounding oddity of this last sentence. Others had grown tired and found a seat. There were even the unfortunate few who had to be singled out and ordered to a cordoned-off spot in the parking lot behind the stadium. Ms. Smith, one of the gym teachers, had staked out a detention area on short notice. She held to her chest a battered clipboard and kept a chewed plastic whistle pressed between her thin lips.

. . . .

When all of the students had finally taken a seat, Mr. Rochambeau smiled and made an announcement. This year, they were going to begin a new tradition. Each grade sat in a distinct section of the bleachers, dividing the main side of the stadium into three parts. Mr. Rochambeau would point to one section. That would be the signal for the chosen grade to make as much noise as possible.

"So who's the best?" Mr. Rochambeau said.

The students looked around, confused.

Mr. Rochambeau shook his head in disgust. "I said, 'So who's the best?'"

Now they understood.

Each of the grades let out screams, hollering and whistling in between gaps of strained fervor. The ninth graders, including Tom and his friends, were convinced they were the leaders of the school. This time was their time, and there was no way they were going to surrender to the younger students, especially the lowly seventh graders. That would be an embarrassment.

Down by the track were special-needs students who had been brought over from the nearby center. They had only just arrived. Some entered the stadium and heard the roar and thought the students were welcoming them. Many of these visiting students were in wheelchairs, their arms one giant mechanism of jerking movements that made them appear robotic and slightly out of control. The remainder of their bodies did not move.

Mr. Rochambeau asked the junior high students in the bleachers above to welcome the visiting students, and this gave the throng yet another opportunity to unleash its collective crowing. Tom cried out, as did those around him. He closed his eyes and screamed louder than he had in a very long time. It felt amazing. Then the sounds fell away, everyone temporarily exhausted.

When Tom opened his eyes, he saw a girl waving at him from near the field. It couldn't be, he thought, but then he remembered his mother telling him earlier that morning. He realized it had been to prepare him.

"Hey, there," Teagan yelled. She was the only one. "Hey, there! Hey, there!" She was standing on her chair and waving up at all of the students. Tom realized she wasn't just waving at him.

Many of the kids started laughing. Then more joined in.

Tom wanted to put his head down.

But he didn't.

He stood up and waved back.

"Tommy!" Teagan said and clapped her hands. She seemed happy enough to cry. One of the teachers nearby guided her back down into her seat. It took some coaxing. Tom continued to stand, suffering the ridicule of his school.

"Young man," Mr. Rochambeau said and pointed excitedly in Tom's direction. "Yes, you there. Report to Ms. Smith, pronto. Hurry up now! You should be ashamed of yourselves."

Tom shook his head, said, "Later," to his friends, and clutched his yearbook as he made his way among the others still sitting. A few rows up, Mario started following him. He had also stood and waved at Teagan, though Tom hadn't seen it.

Mr. Rochambeau continued, "Any other jokers out there want to join them? No? All right, then . . ."

Ms. Smith glanced down at her clipboard and asked for their names. She scanned the columns and then circled each one on the mimeographed list. "Go grab yourself a nice seat of asphalt," she said, replacing the whistle between her lips. Luckily, there was still a good portion of the pavement covered by the shadow of the stadium. Mr. Rochambeau's voice sounded muffled now, as did the screaming of their classmates.

"How long do you think they'll keep us?" Mario said.

Tom didn't answer.

He focused on the other students who sat lined up in front of him, their backs hunched and unmoving, as if the sound of their friends' happiness weighed on them.

"How is she doing?" Mario said.

Tom looked over at him. "You don't talk about her."

Scuffed traffic cones had been placed along the perimeter and formed a barrier separating them from the teachers' cars that were parked in the lot.

"She seemed really happy," Mario offered.

Tom stared hard at Mario and eventually smiled.

"How's your uncle liking jail?" Tom said.

After school, Tom came home to find his father already there. His father had brought home a few empty boxes from the base supply center.

"What are these for, Dad?" Tom said, lightly kicking one of the boxes as he walked into the kitchen. His father mumbled something Tom couldn't understand. He realized too late it was in Tagalog, his father's language. He wished he could remember some of the words, some of the history.

"Sorry, Dad," Tom said.

"Your sister's getting her hair cut," his father said. "When they come back, you should tell her it looks good. Don't forget."

"I saw Teagan today," Tom said.

"You what?"

"I saw her at school. She was at our yearbook signing. I think the center brought her on a field trip or something."

"That doesn't make any sense. Why would she be at your school?"

"Dad, I just told you," Tom said. He watched his father search around the kitchen, looking confused.

"Where did she put it?" his father said, moving some of the things away from the wall. It was obvious to Tom that nothing was hiding behind the squat, lidded containers of flour, sugar, and tea. "Your mother . . ."

"Put *what*, Dad?" Tom said.

"Where did she put my crossword?" he said without turning around. "She is always moving the paper around, you know that, right? I look away for one minute, and it's gone."

Tom checked the kitchen table, but there was only a magazine sitting beside the napkin holder. Then he went over to the empty boxes and peered into one of them. There was a folded newspaper resting at the bottom, though Tom wasn't sure if it was the one his father was looking for.

"One of these days," his father said, "I'm going to have my things in order. You'll see, Tommy. Everything will have a place."

That same evening, Mario stayed in his room and didn't come out until he had memorized most of the periodic table. His parents were bewildered by the student he had become. Mario had heard his chemistry teacher say that anyone looking to go to college would be best served by committing the periodic table to memory. Mr. Sawyer had meant it as a joke. It was supposed to get a reaction, to gauge who was paying attention. The groan from the class would be one indicator. Mario, instead, had written in his notebook, *Memorize the atomic weight of everything.*

May 3, 198–

In regards to: Exequiel X. Guzman
DOC#331VA-77XX

Honorable Members of the Parole Board
Virginia Department of Corrections
P.O. Box 26963
Richmond, VA 23261

Dear Honorable Members of the Parole Board:

My name is Mario Guzman. I am fourteen years old. I
have been a straight-A student at J. E. B. Stuart Junior
High School for three years. I am now finishing the
ninth grade. I am the nephew of Exequiel Guzman
DOC#331VA-77XX. I promised my uncle I would do
well in school. I am keeping my promise.

My uncle is not up for parole, but I thought I would
write to you anyway. If there was some way to consider
him for parole, my family would be grateful. Especially
me. I know he has been working to complete his
GED. He has also told me that he plans to take college
courses, maybe. I think that's great. Don't you think
that's great?

I hope he will be up for parole soon. I don't think he is
guilty for the crime they say he did, but you shouldn't
ask just me. He will tell you he is sorry. My father Paul
Guzman told us the other night the company he works
for is hiring new people. My uncle could be one of those
new people.

I know you can't just let him go. I'm not stupid. But I hope you will think about it. He really, really is a good man. Thank you for taking the time to read my letter to you.

Sincerely,

Mario Guzman

Tom came home from the soccer game. It had been his last for the high school team. All that was left was to prepare for graduation and he could be gone. He found his father in his usual khaki polyester uniform, lying on the couch, having come home early from work. There was an unfinished glass of red wine less than a foot away from his father's draped arm.

Tom paused. His mother had an excuse, at least—she was with Teagan; he could forgive her—but an earlier version of himself would have gone over and kicked the glass, left it for his father to clean up. Or had he ever had the chance to be that kind of kid?

Then the nagging, boyish voice in his head: *How hard would it have been to swing by the school on your way home and catch the last minutes, see your own flesh and blood on the field?*

His father stirred and turned onto his side. His hand brushed the glass. Tom held his breath. The wine nearly spilled, tilting, sloshing slightly, but then didn't.

Tom wished, at the very least, it could have fallen; and now there was the irascible thought blazing up like a phoenix. He couldn't remember his father ever once threatening Exequiel Guzman.

Years ago, when Tom had been in the courtroom, watching the trial move slowly from question to question, exhibit to exhibit, never once did his father stand up, as Tom had wanted him to, and hurl a chair at the man sitting silently and staring at his hands. Never once did his father scream at Exequiel Guzman.

There was none of that.

There was just one man doing nothing to the one man who had already done everything.

. . . .

Around the living room were small piles of things, especially magazines and newspapers. His father had been declaring that almost everything was necessary. His mother disagreed. There had been fights over the gathering presence, but mostly, his mother conceded. Items were beginning to pile and lean against one another, like the motionless barges along the Elizabeth, the still river cleaving the city.

His father turned onto his other side, facing Tom.

His eyes opened.

"What are you doing here?"

"The game's over," Tom said.

"What game?"

"My soccer game, Dad. My last game."

"Oh."

Tom had not changed out of his own uniform. The gold jersey was covered in grass stains. Tom had not peeled away the shin guards that were streaked with mud, small proof that he at one point had actually fought for something. Even if that ball, wrapped in all of its ephemeral beauty, felt wholly insignificant now.

He could check items off his mental list, counting down the remaining responsibilities he had as a graduating senior. It was not for him to be the kind of son his father would dote on. He wasn't going to play at the University of Virginia, he wasn't that good.

"So who won, Tommy?" his father said, closing his eyes.

"I guess we did."

Tom didn't explain how he was already beginning to remove himself, how he was no longer thinking of his high school team with any sense of loyalty. And he wasn't going to mention to his father how he had been the last to take a penalty shot, how the net had pulled taut from the momentum, catching the ball, and he had stood there stoic, frozen like a statue, while a wave of strangers came rushing toward him.

Manny Serafino dreamt of Fely, the one girl in his school who knew more English than even the teachers. Her grandfather was an American soldier from Tennessee who had come to the Philippine Islands at the turn of the century to fight Filipinos. But after the war, he had stayed behind. Fely used to smile and say it was because of love.

"He had only glimpsed my lola," she said to Manny. "And he was smitten with her."

"Smitten?" Manny said. He didn't know this word.

"It means *to be taken with someone.*"

This didn't help.

"Enamored," Fely tried again.

"Oh, right," Manny said. Then he said the word *love* in Tagalog. She laughed at his pronunciation, so American-sounding now.

Even though he was dreaming, he licked his hand and wiped the back of his hair. The part his own lola used to call stubborn.

"I wonder if you will remember me," Fely said.

"Why do you say it that way?" he said. "I'm remembering you now."

"When you get older, you will leave for the States and marry someone else and never come back."

"That's not true," Manny said, but then he realized it was. He loved Elinor, but his younger self remained with Fely. He could see her as she would be now, older. Slender. Her black hair all one length, tied back and resting between her shoulder blades. The hair not cropped and fashionable.

There was also the fact that she was mestiza. She had her grandfather Frank from Knoxville to thank for her straight nose, her hazel eyes.

"After you left, some evenings I would sit by the water and just listen for fish," she said. "The startled ones surfacing. Splashing the moon into pieces. I would sit there and wait. The image always surprised me."

"How could you do such a thing?" Manny asked.

She didn't care that he would be confused by her story.

"I needed to see things come back together," Fely said.

With that, she vanished.

Manny woke with the vague recollection that his son had been standing in front of him wearing a bright gold jersey. A number in the upper-right corner of the jersey, like one of the squares of his crossword puzzles, the emptiness of his son mocking him.

When Manny closed his eyes, he returned to Fely, but he had willed it this time.

"Do me a favor," she said.

"Yes."

"Don't come back for me."

"You don't understand," he said.

"It doesn't matter."

"I had an opportunity to leave, and so I did. The money I made, I sent most of it home. My brother went to the university because of this money. My mother and father could finally make ends meet."

"It would have happened without you," she said and unfastened her hair.

He didn't move.

He watched strands fall in long black lines. Blank music sheets, scores never written.

"When I was living in California for that brief time, no one would look at me," he said. "My friends, yes, but on leave from the base, I would walk the streets downtown and most of the young pretty women I saw would never meet my eye."

"You were thinking about me."

"Yes."

"You would see their passing reflections in the storefronts."

"Yes, in the glass."

"You would think you saw me and then would turn around, only to find that I wasn't there. I was never there."

"How did you do that?"

"What do you mean?"

"How could you appear and disappear that way?" he said.

"I was going to ask you the same thing," she said.

It had not been a dream, though it had felt like one. Fely in his arms as they lay in the shallow boat and drifted out beyond the breakers. In the distance, they could hear faint explosions, and Manny knew his cousin Tranquilino and a gang of boys were throwing sticks of dynamite into the sea. Floating among the cluttered chunks of loosened coral was the occasional stunned fish, its yellow stripes blazing like flames on the water's surface.

"He's going to hurt himself," Fely said, without looking at Manny. The silence on the water was a line of deep blue he could snag, even with the boat's meager anchor, and pull to them.

"We should go back," he said.

He thought he had seen a fin, triangular and dark.

"Why? The only things there are the same things. Your loud cousin. Your aunties' wretched voices singing while they do their chores by the river."

Manny laughed now.

"It's terrible," Fely said. "It's a crime, really."

"Where would we go then?"

She sat up, keeping one hand in his lap, and looked around. He wondered if she was aware of how close she was, how easily she could be seen. Back in town, she would have to lie to her family. She had been on a boat alone with Manny Serafino. *Hindi, hindi. God, no.*

She lay back against him, holding her arms out so that her fingers gripped the sides.

"I don't care where we go," she said, exasperated.

In the distance, another explosion.

"I can't take you if you don't tell me where," he said.

She sighed. Her back pressed harder into him, her eyes softening. She sat up and turned around, grabbing the sides of the boat again, rocking this time.

"What are you doing?" he said.

"We'll fake our deaths."

"What?"

She said it again.

The boat dipped to one side and then slid back. The sloshing caused it to take on water. It was thirsty, wanting the ocean.

"Stop it," he said.

"What's wrong?" she said, laughing. "You're a good swimmer. You can pull me to shore, can't you? They'll find the boat. They'll assume we're dead."

Near the far edge of the island, they could see his cousin and the other boys coming around the bend. Before Manny could say anything else, she threw her weight in a jolt to one side. The boat dropped down and filled with a rush, as if a giant hand were pushing the gunwale toward the sea's depths.

He and Fely both fell in.

The boat sprang back, righting itself, and then floated away. They both surfaced.

Manny frantically searched the water.

Fely laughed, squealing.

She was happy she had surprised him. He needed that.

"There's a shark," he said.

"Where?" she said. "I don't think so."

"Somewhere," he said.

She swam over to him and put her arms around his neck. She whispered into his ear. He nodded, even though he was furious at her. Their boat had floated a good distance. He knew his cousin would spot it and bring it back.

The water was clear. She swam ahead of him. He watched her body, her legs noodling. He rose to take a breath. The shore was far away. He descended. She rose and he paused, floating underneath her, and watched how the cloth of her shirt grew undulant before she surfaced. From the spot where he was now, he could see sparkling lines ahead.

At first, he thought they were ghosts, shapes outlining swaths of silk-like material, shimmering purple and blue and white. Wedding dresses thrown into the sea. Floating in their emptiness. He thought he could see a processional in the way the shapes were lining up. He thought of the stories his lola had told him, *ang mga aswang,* evil spirits that roamed the islands, vampires and demons waiting to grab you at any moment.

Fely swam ahead of him again.

This time he chased her. He wanted to grab her legs and pull her back.

The shapes, he could see now, were of this world. Box jellyfish, fluffy and translucent. Fely had gone too close. In turning to come back toward him, she had kicked her leg out and grazed one long, beaded strand. Nematocysts anchored her. Though she was able to swim free of the tentacle, the poison drew her back. It pulled her breath into a shallow place.

Manny grabbed her and lifted her into the air. If he were to head toward the shore now, he would have to navigate through the sudden colony. Behind him, the boat was a dash. His cousin and the other boys were mere silhouettes warbling. They could have been gulls buoyant on the surface.

All he knew was that Fely was swallowing water. She was trying to say something, but winced instead, as if the words were barbed, catching in her throat.

She was crying. Manny kissed her face and said, "I'm here, I'm here," and he thought her breathing was slowing so he screamed toward the distant shadows, lifting one arm as high as it would go, and the distant shadows screamed back.

Mario had just graduated from high school and had taken it upon himself to go alone. It had scared him. His mother and father wanted nothing to do with the man they had taken into their home, who had given them nothing in return but years full of glares from the community. That and hate mail. Crank calls equally venomous and at all hours. Mario remembered those the most.

He went to a parole board interview. He didn't know the rules. He sat quietly behind a small table in the middle of a poorly lit room as, from a distance, a large black woman with a lazy eye gazed back at him. She smiled to reveal a violent smear of dark lipstick stuck to her tiny front teeth, settled in the grooves.

"Son, what is your relationship to the inmate . . . Exequiel Guzman?" the woman said. She pronounced his uncle's name *Execute All Goosemen.*

"I'm his nephew," Mario said.

The woman shook her head.

"I'm afraid you're not allowed to . . ."

"I just need to tell you a little bit about my uncle," he interrupted.

He could feel the words. He had read them countless times, folded and refolded the pages so that they fit into the front pocket of his pants. He ran his finger over the blistered papers where they now rested in case he should need to refer to them again.

"When I was a boy, my uncle Exequiel came to live with us. It won't mean anything for me to say this now, but he saved my life."

The woman leaned forward so that the gray foam head of the microphone on the desk covered her mouth completely. Then her voice filled the room with clipped static: "Son, I'm afraid . . ."

Mario didn't hesitate now.

"A bunch of us were out playing in the street, and this car comes flying around the corner. Its headlights were busted, I think. I don't know.

The point is, you couldn't see it coming. No one could. Especially me. I was standing there in the middle of the street, and my uncle comes out of nowhere and just pushes me out of the way."

"That was very brave," the woman said.

"It was," he said, looking down. "It was."

"Son?"

"Yes?" Mario said.

"Are you finished?"

The woman was still smiling, and there was something about her tone that made Mario feel her curiosity was put on. He had known it the moment he walked in the room, when he had shaken her padded hand and the padded hands of the other parole board members. In her, though, he had sensed it immediately, that *it wasn't going to happen*, which is why Mario had stopped his rehearsed story halfway through.

He'd had it all planned out, had worked up how the car would have thrown his uncle's body into the sky, and how the limp each of the parole examiners had surely seen, or would see eventually, might be connected to this moment of sacrifice. It would unfold perfectly. So much so that it was a story Mario felt he could continue to carry with him after this day. It felt real.

It had almost happened that way, he told himself, or if he had truly been standing there and a car had been careening toward him, he knew his uncle would not have hesitated and would have rushed into the street to save him.

"The car missed him," Mario said finally, wiping his eyes.

"Do you need a minute, son?"

"Thank you," Mario said.

He rubbed his sleeve across his face.

The woman put her hand over the microphone, but Mario could still hear her words. "He really shouldn't be here," she said to a pinkish, splotchy-skinned white man sitting to her left. His eyes fluttered like peeling paint on a fence post, where barbed wire had rusted through. The man lifted his face from the folder he had been inspecting. He had been reading with his eyes close to the words and images, studying the collage of evidence. He kept regarding the picture of a young girl, the clear line of sutures that resembled two continents coming together. *Plate tectonics.*

He had helped his own daughter with her homework weeks before, and the lesson was fresh in his mind. Then the photo of Exequiel Guzman after he was arrested, his withdrawn glare and the stooped way he held his body within the frame—that and the photocopy of the smudged fingerprints, squiggly lines that appeared to avoid one another for a short time just before their collision. They could have been symbols for water on a map. Rivers bunched together, then running their separate ways into the sea.

Mario went home and told his parents. He had gone to the parole board hearing even though he wasn't supposed to, and he told them he was sorry. At first, they thought he was talking about how he had lied to them and taken the car so far away when he knew he shouldn't have.

He could not bring himself to say it at first.

His mother held his face to keep him still.

"You think he had nothing to do with it?" his mother said.

"Had nothing to do with *what?*" his father said. The man's eyes widened.

Mario could barely breathe.

"What are you saying, *mijo?*" his father said.

"I don't know," Mario said.

"Yes, you do," his mother said. "Take it slow. Start from the beginning."

Mario began to sob, but his father would have none of it. He looked as if he would punch the wall his son was leaning against. He looked as if he would take apart the house with his hands.

"Tell us," his mother said.

His father said nothing now.

Mario took a breath and told them what neither could believe.

Tom's original thought had been to take it slow, wade into the experience before committing to a club or even a major. He thought he might want to be either a lawyer or a doctor of some sort; however, after orientation, he realized the majority of the students he had met had similar aspirations. There would be work to do. To make matters worse, most had been valedictorians or salutatorians of their graduating classes, and common sense dictated that if all of them followed through on this shared dream, there would hardly be room left for him.

His first night on campus, though, had proved too exciting. Just getting ready to go to the dining hall could be an event. He meandered with others who lived in his dormitory. Just a first year in a gang of other first years. They wandered the grounds in new orange or navy-blue T-shirts with clever Wahoo sayings and looked to meet other students, to see what was going on. Around them, a force field of Polo and Drakkar emanated.

There were the numerous, banal questions one had to answer. Questions that felt attached to a rhetorical merry-go-round, specifically designed to accommodate both the person asking the question and the one having to provide a response. Instead of lacquered, colorfully painted horses, there was the inquiry, "So where are you from?" or "What kind of bands do you like?"

Tom met Rachel the first week. When he walked into the party, she pointed right at him and at first, he didn't get it. Then she walked over and said, "Nice shirt." She was wearing the same one he had on. Before he could respond, she started in on other questions he had already answered throughout the day. Someone on his floor had thrown together this party, replete with grain punch and stacked cases of Milwaukee's Beast.

He didn't tell her he was from Norfolk. He felt it would be better if he just said, "the beach." Norfolk being close enough in his mind, and she said she thought that was cool. It turned out she was from Northern Virginia, but she called it *NoVa,* a word he had never heard associated with the region. She had three older brothers, all of whom had graduated from here. With a slight pout, she added she was sad she couldn't bring her puppy Rufus to live with her. Maybe next year, once she could grab a place off campus. Tom suspected Rufus had been a gift from a boyfriend back in Occoquan.

"What about you?" she said. "Do you have any brothers or sisters?"

He looked around the room. Everyone was happy, smiling.

"No," he said evenly. "Only child."

"That's sad," Rachel said and made a point of frowning.

And there it was. His new life.

Tom lay in her loft-style bed and studied a shadow on the ceiling. A desk lamp had been left on. He thought maybe her roommate was up early, but when he leaned over the side to search the room, he found it empty.

He could tell by Rachel's steady breathing that she had drifted off. She was still in her jeans and J. Crew blouse, her suede buck shoes and socks the only things she'd discarded. It felt practiced to him, this controlled abandon, but then she started jerking slightly, her legs mostly.

He remembered how he and Teagan, when they were really little, used to sit on the living room floor while their parents huddled together on the couch. The television would be on, and the family dog, a shepherd-hound mix, would be sprawled out near the set, dreaming. The dog's legs would kick in sleep as if trying to function. To run. Tom and Teagan would cup their mouths to contain the bursts of laughter. With bodies shuddering, they would both look back at their parents on the couch, who would also be holding back. In that moment, there would be a shared secret as they all watched the dog chasing the invisible thing.

Only when the dog became so engrossed that there was yelping did he and Sissy drop their hands and laugh loudly. Tom pounded the floor. He couldn't help it. The dog looked confused. It had been startled, stunned by the laughter. Teagan would be the one to apologize and nuzzle the dog's muzzle, rubbing its soft ears and whispering, "We're sorry, Pilot. We're sorry," until the laughter died down and there was still Teagan, consoling for having taken the dog away from its dream. No one in the room spoke; they just wiped their eyes because it had been too much, their happiness.

It was not sadness now. He had felt that before, been consumed by it actually. He watched this girl sleep, the girl whom he had met in the city of his new life.

Days later, on his way to his Introduction to American History class, he was approached on campus by a third year. His name was Chase and he wore a crushed baseball cap sporting Greek letters and covering a spray of sandy blond curls. His blue Oxford had been unbuttoned just so to reveal a tight, surfer necklace of bleached white shells.

Chase was from the same hometown as Tom's roommate, Landon, somewhere in the western part of the state. Chase asked Tom if he had considered rushing a fraternity, and when Tom just shrugged, not wanting to appear one way or the other, Chase grinned and said he understood and handed Tom a slip of paper with a scrawled address. Tom had just read a chapter on the whaling vessels of the Northeast, could still picture the inset of a piece of scrimshaw.

"A couple of guys are meeting up to watch the Skins," Chase said. "You and Landon should stop by. But just you two, okay? Is that cool?"

"Cool," Tom said, and with that, Chase tipped his hat and blended in with the others milling about the crowded corridor.

That evening, Tom went alone. All of the guys there wore similar baseball hats, the same Greek letters. Rather than turning around and leaving, Tom ended up staying and drinking with them, cheering mindlessly whenever Riggins plowed into the end zone. Later in the week, there were more events, more opportunities to *get wasted,* as Chase liked to scream and the other brothers would holler back in response.

When Tom was given a bid to pledge the fraternity, it was not a surprise. He had expected it. Chase himself delivered the bid in the same spot, outside his Introduction to American History class, the only class so far that Tom was beginning to like.

At the chapter house on Rugby Road, he stood with his new pledge brothers. He couldn't help thinking about the other guys he had seen during rush events. Those who had tried their hardest to please, it turned out they were the ones who didn't get a bid. Tom knew it was a game, but he didn't care.

A kid who announced himself as the pledge master pinned a star on Tom's T-shirt. Tom wished then he had worn something a little more formal. The other pledges all seemed to have taken note of the same memo explaining the dress code: buttoned-up blue Oxford shirt, woven leather belt, khakis, a frayed UVA baseball hat. When Tom raised his hand like the others and recited the same words, he could feel his voice falling away.

At the first real pledging activity, Tom balanced on top of a metal folding chair. There were his other pledge brothers doing the same thing; the sound of creaking filled the room. Tom then covered his face while the brothers in the fraternity began to shout obscenities and hurl old food at him.

The night before, he had been in the same corner making out with a girl whose hair, even in the smoky atmosphere, smelled like strawberries. Now he was covered in cold oatmeal and pea soup. One of his pledge brothers was smeared with a concoction of cottage cheese and kidney beans, another with mustard and slices of lunchmeat. More food flew past him. It made no sense, which was the point.

"You suck!" the brothers screamed. "You're worthless!"

Tom began to flinch with each hit.

"You'll never be a brother!" they said.

And so he never was.

four

*P*rior offenses? It was not said this way. Those who spoke to him sometimes asked, and Shoe could not list them. Or would not list them. He suffered heavily for not speaking, for not finding the words.

Everywhere he looked there were words.

Scratched on the walls, inside the rims of sinks and steel commodes. Even on the arms of men. Smeared words. Colorful scripts. There was no shortage of language and the bodies of men that carried all forms of phrases, chants, and prayers blended with glistening skin.

He began to read poems in the prison library. He committed one to memory.

At any one time the yard was alive with language carried on backs widening with splayed lats, tattooed knuckles tightening over bars wrapped in worn cloth tape. Someone straining to lift the weight, a word there in their hands. A word like his nephew's name scrawled in the air. It moved from neck to neck, arm to arm, until it landed in Shoe's mouth and he whispered it to himself before crossing the yard.

Sometimes he made it across without anyone noticing his slow walk, his foot dragging behind him. Sometimes he pretended to be normal, untouched by his circumstances, and in those moments, he was the most scared. It would not last, and he could feel it, this life fading in and out. His prior life.

And sometimes he thought about Elle in Taos, the last time they had spoken, and what had become of her son. He thought about this boy and Mario and himself. And what of his own childhood? Had he done the right thing, ever?

She had not been his first choice, though in the crowded setting he could already tell she was taller than he was and blonde, two features he had discovered he liked in particular, and when she wandered off from the other women in her corner booth and disappeared to the back of the bar, Exequiel left the torn cushioned stool where he had been watching her and slipped among the other stragglers, all red and blue flannel shirts and jeans, bodies shadowy as open water, and went in search of her.

The cigarette machine, with its colorful labels and worn plastic pull levers, resembled a thrown-together robot, angled as it was with its mirrored-finish metal trim catching blue and green lights splashing from the stage where a band was struggling through a cover of The Eagles' "Take It Easy." Every so often one of the waitresses would join in on the chorus.

He passed the pool table. Off to the side were two men dressed in the similar stamped country-western attire, flannel and jeans, but with rigid bolo ties and clean cowboy hats as accents. They were sipping on beers and nodding at nothing in particular, pushing around the cue ball like it was bothering them.

The ball zigzagged across the field of scuffed felt and then returned only to be shoved harder. It came back that much harder the next time. Momentum accrued from their impatience, more nods and shoving of the cue ball, until the two men took notice of the one walking past, dragging his foot behind him. The smaller of the two, with his round, penny-colored face, said, "Hey, bud, you fall off your bull or something?" and the taller friend laughed and nodded as he took a long swig from his bottle, its glass the color of wet pine bark.

"Hey, friend, Lee asked you a question," the taller one said.

Exequiel stopped at the edge of the table and grabbed the cue, lifting it up so that he interrupted its course. "I'm not your friend, *puta*,"

Exequiel said, making sure he eyed both of the men. They looked to him like off-duty rodeo clowns, men who should otherwise be wearing makeup and polka-dotted pants ten sizes too big with hula hoops for waistbands, all of it held up by fat pairs of matching suspenders.

Exequiel took a slow breath and then said, "Sorry," and at this, the smaller one, Lee, smiled and came around the side of the table and said, "Oh, now don't piss yourself, bud. What was that you said? What did you say? Roger and me didn't quite get that last bit there."

"Yeah," Roger said.

"I said I'm sorry," Exequiel said, staring into the cue ball like it was a crystal ball. Something a dwarf fortune teller might use. He looked hard into its milky core but could find only some traces of blue smeared in erratic streaks on the surface. Its life consisting of hits.

"*Sorry?* Sorry for what?" Roger said. He hadn't moved and stood where he was, sipping his beer. When he started to walk around, his smaller friend held up his hand to stop him.

"Yeah, bud," Lee said. "What would you be sorry for?"

He was happy that this stranger was the kind of man who would take Roger and him seriously. He was happier, too, that the near-stoic look on this stooped man's face might be masking a rising fear. Lee wondered what they could get him to do, what strange routine this man they had stopped would suddenly perform for the two of them. Would he buy them both a round for the inconvenience, maybe? Or maybe he would buy a round for everyone within earshot, beers for the women in the back corner booth and beers for the men, this stranger with a sheepish grin and scraggly mustache, his strange way of crossing a room, beers for the band? Even a shot of whiskey for the pretty blonde leaving the restroom?

When Exequiel looked up he saw the woman pause, assessing him and the others. Exequiel didn't care. He asked her if she knew these guys. Perhaps it was the way she reacted, scoffing almost, that sent fire through him, a goring that burned in his blood and washed over his chest like that same blood burning.

Gaslit grass gone in one gush of wind.

His eyes watering from the smoke inside him.

Not that Exequiel could have known this woman's past, but he sensed in her a reckless stretch of judgment. Rather than laughing off his proposition of a whiskey shot, she stood closer to Exequiel and leaned on him to get a better look, as if to peer into the future the cue ball held inside.

She whispered, "You shouldn't let them get to you."

"I know," he said. "I'm sorry."

"Don't do that. You haven't done anything yet."

"Yet?"

"Yes," she said. "You know what that means, don't you?"

He left her to move closer to Lee, the smaller one. Once Exequiel was within an arm's length, he grabbed Lee's throat. His thumb threatening to snap the larynx altogether. He felt it give, but then it slid back without breaking. The trauma alone, though, caused the smaller man to collapse onto the table. It was then Exequiel began to shove the cue ball into the man's mouth. He was bloodying the teeth and the lips, trying to get it inside him, trying to get him to suck it like an egg.

"Hey," Roger said, confused. "Hey, friend! What are you doing, friend?"

Lee, the smaller one, had passed out.

Exequiel thought at first he was going to have to break the friend Roger's cheek, especially if he tried to interfere now, but the friend Roger remained in place, as if paralyzed. Better yet, as if his boots were nailed to the floor.

Roger would make a terrible rodeo clown. They both would.

Before anyone could make sense of the scene, the woman pulled Exequiel through the back exit and into the parking lot. A film lay over the stars in the Taos night sky, as if the sky were packaged. A store-bought cosmos.

Across the road was a field of sagebrush. Tumbleweed rolled like ghost cue balls roaming the pocked felt. The yellow lights from nearby adobe houses were brighter than the stars themselves.

"What's your name?" Exequiel said.

"Elle," the woman said. "Why?"

"I don't know," he said and then kissed her.

She kissed him back.

"What's your name?" she said, pulling away finally, smiling. She was embarrassed.

"Jeff," he said.

"That's bullshit. What is it?"

"Jeremy."

"Now you're just fucking with me."

"I am?"

She laughed.

He seemed different from the recent ones. A part of her was still burning from the encounter she had witnessed. She wanted to return to the bar and see him do it again. She almost said for them to go back inside. She wanted to see what he would do if he had to own up to the damage he had done.

"I don't think we should stay out here any longer," she said, scanning the parking lot. "What do you drive?"

"I don't."

"Here," she said and took his hand. It was warm.

It wasn't until she was leaning against the door of her Chevelle that she realized it was the same hand. The one that had held the cue ball almost lovingly at first. Or so it had seemed to her.

Before he smashed it, mashing and smashing again, on the guy's mouth.

His frayed way of saying, "Is this what you wanted? Is this what you want? Is it? *Sit?*"

Before Elle was born, her father had worked as a smoke jumper for the U.S. Forest Service in Okanogan County, Washington. Elle and her younger brother Wallace grew up hearing lots of stories about their father's former life. It was almost too much to imagine. Even so, each night the stories would begin in a vivid burst, their father young again, beaming as he described the rush of being aloft and drifting down through billowy tents of smoke.

During such stories, Wallace would be busy giggling. Elle, on the other hand, would almost always drift off into sleep, already thinking of what lay underneath those dark sheets of smoke pulled taut by gusts: dancing horses, bejewelled and riderless, spinning in brilliant circles, and those horses turning easily into spun shadows. Images, for Elle, sweet as cotton candy. Sometimes her brother's giggling broke the dream.

Until their father had met his wife, Marsha, and settled down in nearby Winthrop, Samuel Lufkin had spent his life looking for an opportunity to make an impact. He had just missed serving in the war, and everywhere he went, banners in storefronts stretching jubilant phrases, newspapers in succession printing the same victorious stories, he was reminded how he hadn't been needed at all. He could just as easily have vanished into the surrounding wilderness and the country would have continued on in its history of having won the war without him.

This was Samuel Lufkin's dilemma, the kind of thing that kept him up nights in his own parents' house thinking of how it was he wanted to be remembered. When he first learned there was a training facility nearby, he knew what he had to do. He signed up to become a smoke jumper. Five years he jumped out of planes, risking his life to put out the flames of mindless fires.

Fire, the head of the Lufkin family preached each night, *does not know it is evil.*

For this reason, it seemed worse to Elle. It was no different from the monsters in the stories she had already read as a girl. The many heads of the Hydra. The way cutting off one side caused the flames to split into two directions. In the scenes her father described, she sometimes pictured the flames rejoining to flicker like a large forked tongue.

Years in this line of work had given Samuel Lufkin an appreciation for the mere fact of being alive. He realized that who he had been before was a child caught in his own yearning. And he was surprised that he didn't care how, after a few years of marriage, his life took on a routine, his days consisting mostly of pumping gas and running a cash register at the service station, or the occasional minor challenge of setting points for a tune-up in the adjoining garage.

Samuel and Marsha were pleased with the quiet, consistent life they had given their daughter and son. Their routine afforded them a certain kind of stability that suited the people they had naturally become. Bills were paid on time. Meals were always on the table. Sundays after church had, out of a joyful habit, become outings at Pearrygin Lake. Bodies cradled in huge inner tubes Samuel had saved from the garage spun aimlessly across the lake's surface. Here clouds drifted just as slowly among the reflected images of willows and ash of the Methow Valley.

During these tuck-in stories, though, what Samuel Lufkin had failed each night to explain to his children was the reason he had given up on being a smoke jumper in the first place. In the woven fabric of their family lore, it was known, by Elle especially, how their mother Marsha had spotted him, the young Sam, *dashing* in his uniform. He had been stepping off a Greyhound bus. Marsha and her best friend in high school, a girl named Esther whom the children had grown up never meeting, had flipped a coin over who was going to talk to the boy with the bright eyes. Who was going to ask him for his name?

Elle always remembered thinking how uncharacteristically brave her mother seemed for approaching this stranger from elsewhere. Elle, as a young girl, could never imagine doing such a thing. Not then at least.

"He must have been so handsome," Elle would often offer as a prompt, and her mother would laugh in disbelief and respond, "Yes, yes, oh yes." She would clap her hands together, as if trying to catch the elusive image. She could have been a girl herself, cupping the air to trap the first lightning bug aglow in the evening.

"Oh, Elle, you should have seen him then," her mother would say, walking into the room with freshly folded clothes and setting them down next to each child's dresser, then kissing her husband on the cheek. She would leave so that he could finish his story before Wallace asked for another glass of water, or Elle tried to get them to begin an impromptu waltz, something they would claim they had danced at their wedding. Of course their daughter knew then that there had been no celebration, only the visit to a justice of the peace and a stiff handshake from her grandfather Roy, her mother's father.

"Here's the thing," Samuel Lufkin started out once. "You never know how much sky you can hold inside you. Until you try, I mean. Go ahead, Elle. Take a breath." He wanted to bring his children always to that moment of drifting, the parachute a translucent dome overhead.

For Elle, sometimes the parachute was a fading hand collecting the wind.

When Elle went away to college and briefly studied art history, what she felt seemed to her more than a simple affinity for spaces held in the ceilings of basilicas. It was the sculpted infinity within each apse that lifted her, that promised another dimension to the faith in life her parents had provided her. The family settling in for the night, she and her brother listening to their father's voice while the rest of Winthrop prepared for sleep as well. And in her memory, she could still see the reddish fused fingers of her father's left hand peeking out from a sleeve. That hand gliding down and whipping about, like a leaf in a storm. Tailspun and drifting. Then gently, always gently, and punctuated with such patience, the idea of bringing back to life one's former self.

When the Chevelle pulled into the driveway, its tires displaced the gravel easily, even though there were sizable chunks, flotsam of larger rock pulverized for domestic use. The car slid to a quiet stop, but just barely, and Elle thought for a moment of the way the bottom of a canoe can smooth water underneath with the flatness of its hull.

Exequiel spotted in the cast glow up ahead a woman lying on a couch in the front room, the long window like a television screen broadcasting another fictitious life. When Exequiel turned back to Elle, the woman he had just met in the bar, he found she had been the one, in fact, watching him. She was studying his expression to glean how he might be taking in the scene of the one sprawled, passed out.

"Can you tell if she's sleeping?" Elle whispered to Exequiel.

He shrugged.

Elle leaned over to kiss his neck, just as he happened to turn his face. Their lips brushed each other. It was awkward. Elle smiled, trying to hold back from laughing altogether. He did the same.

She sensed something about this man. That he was kind. Or kinder than others she had known, especially since she had been a single mother. There was not any one thing she could point to that would justify her feeling this way, especially so quickly, but just this conscious thought in her head, that he was *a kind man,* made her want to laugh out loud.

How had she become so pathetic?

She needed to be more mysterious. Bringing him back to her house seemed dangerous. Or worse, desperate. It wasn't the kind of thing she needed to be doing anyway. She shuddered hearing the tone of her mother's voice as she said it in just that way, telling Elle that she'd had more opportunities than she, her mother, ever had. *Just look at what you've made of yourself.*

. . . .

"Who is she?" Exequiel said.

Elle hesitated.

She gazed at the window. In the haze of the room, the older woman sprawled on the couch. Her nightgown open some. Nothing was showing. Elle wished there could have been something, at least.

Elle knew there was a knife. It was hidden, used as a bookmark. The Bible, with its tattered leather cover and gilded onionskin pages, rested on the floor next to the couch.

"One time I scared my mom so good," Elle said, biting her lip.

"Scared her?"

"Yeah, I tiptoed up to the window and then banged on the glass as hard as I could. She said I almost gave her a heart attack."

Elle laughed and shook her head.

"Isn't that funny?" she said, wiping her eyes.

"Why would you do that to your mother?" he said.

Her laughter trailed off. She smiled.

The man beside her was becoming someone else. It was almost too easy, the way it could occur. How he could stop being the kind man she had met in the bar, whom she had driven here in her car. The man she had allowed herself to be foolish in front of and not care how she appeared to him.

Maybe he wasn't so different from the others.

It could be Joshua, her son's father, sitting beside her now. If that were the case, Elle knew she would already have slipped the house key into the front door. She would have gone inside, stepping along quietly so as not to surprise her mother, and she would have reached down for the Bible and opened the book and found the knife hidden there and seen, before standing back up in the artificial glow, a line from Psalms. The one about the valley of the shadow of death. Her mother's favorite. Elle would have used that knife to cut away every memory Joshua still had of her and their son.

Seeing again the stranger beside her, she leaned into him and said, "I'm sorry." He did not respond with words. He nodded at the quiet surrounding the car. At the image of the woman's mother asleep on the couch. The television continued to wash her body in bluish neon.

"You're welcome to stay the night," Elle said. "Or should I take you home?"

"I don't care," he said to her.

She put the car in reverse and backed out of the driveway. A street-light had smoothed out its small, yellow dress over the distant inter-section, where other cars were parked crooked near the curb. She let the car idle.

She was staring ahead.

"Where are you from anyway?" she said.

"Nowhere."

"Really," she said. "Where are you from?"

"A bunch of places."

"Name one."

"I don't remember their names."

"You make them sound like women."

He laughed.

"What?" she said.

"I wish," he said.

When he woke, Exequiel could smell coconut. That and oranges. The blended scent had stirred him from his slumber. He rubbed his eyes to see a boy sitting on the bed and observing him. The boy had an angry cowlick curling above the back of his head. It looked like the top of a question mark.

"Who are you?" the boy said.

"Exequiel," he said, trying to sound American.

"What does that mean? Your name means something, doesn't it?"

"You must be Wendell."

"No," the boy said and shook his head. The scent of coconut fell on Exequiel again, and he realized it was the boy's hair, the tropical fragrance of the shampoo.

As his eyes adjusted, Exequiel could see that the sides of the boy's hair were still damp, fresh from a morning bath.

"So you're *not* Wendell?" Exequiel said, squinting.

Exequiel pretended he could not hide his confusion very well and pinched lightly at the bridge of his nose. The boy sensed this play. He cupped his mouth to keep from showing the wide gaps in his teeth.

"I'm kidding," the boy said.

"Oh, I see. You're a jokester."

The boy nodded quickly, happy to be given this title.

"Where's your mother?" Exequiel said.

"Making breakfast. Do you like eggs?"

"I love eggs."

"Well, we don't have any eggs."

Exequiel laughed.

"Do you like cereal?" the boy said.

"No," Exequiel said. "I don't."

"Well, that's too bad. That's all we have."

"How long have you been playing?" Exequiel said, sliding the rook across the chessboard.

Wendell took his pawn and moved it five spaces. Exequiel could see rules meant nothing to this boy.

"I haven't been playing long, just my whole life," the boy yawned.

"Well, I can tell," Exequiel said.

"What's that supposed to mean?"

Without waiting for Exequiel to make a next move, the boy picked up his king and slid the piece five spaces. He placed the king alongside the pawn he had just moved.

"That's his dad," Wendell said. "They go everywhere together."

"Oh," Exequiel said. He nodded, a serious expression.

The boy told him that the chess set had belonged to his grandfather, who had been a firefighter and had died. He was quick to explain that his grandfather didn't die being a smoke jumper.

"He was lucky," the boy said. "He died from being old."

Exequiel didn't know what a smoke jumper was, but thought perhaps it had to do with the circus. As the boy spoke, Exequiel's mind wandered to a time when he had seen one. He had been amazed to watch a woman swallow swords. A bald, heavyset man had danced around the ring and breathed fire. The air in front of the audience filled with white plumes of smoke.

Maybe this man had been a smoke jumper?

"What's that anyway?" Exequiel said.

"What?"

"*Smoke jumper.*"

"I don't really know," the boy said without looking up. He put his finger on top of another pawn's helmet and didn't take it off.

"Maybe your mom knows?" Exequiel said.

"I should hope so," the boy said. "It was her father after all."

"We should ask her."

"Good luck," the boy said. "She's secretive."

"What does that mean? *Secretive.*"

"I don't know," the boy said. "Grandmarsha likes to use that word."

The boy spoke with a trained solemnity, but then couldn't hold back any longer. He started laughing, baring his smile. Exequiel could see the teeth were coming in crooked.

"There's another way you can play this game, but you can't move the pieces around so much. Did you know that?" Exequiel said.

The boy stopped smiling.

"I didn't mean to offend you," Exequiel said.

"You didn't *offend* me," the boy said.

"I think I did."

"No."

Wendell called for his mother, who was in the back of the house. She yelled back, asking him what he wanted. He wanted to tell her this man could leave their house now. How long was he going to stay anyway?

He was angry at his mother and at himself.

Did this man think for one minute he was going to come in here and change the rules of this game? Did he not realize that the chessboard had been a gift from his grandfather?

Was this man, whatever his stupid name meant, so stupid that he didn't understand how things worked around here? Was he really *that* stupid?

When Exequiel returned to the house, it was early evening. The day still clung to his clothes. Sweat and sawdust and plaster mix. He could taste the chemical tinge on the back of his tongue. He couldn't help thinking there was something about this work, after all was said and done, that was bad for the body. He'd give it a few more weeks, tops.

Wendell was in the front yard throwing a baseball in the air. A bat lay on the ground next to him. His grandmother sat in a busted chair on the front porch and leaned over and tapped her ashes into an empty glass. She cut her eyes at Exequiel as he approached.

"Would you like some tea?" she said. "I just made some."

"Thank you," he said.

He had almost said it in Spanish. Not that it would have been bad to have done so. Elle's mother had told him, on numerous occasions, that he reminded her of the actor Ricardo Montalban. He never admitted he didn't know who that was.

"Wend, would you want some tea?" she said to the boy.

Wendell nodded, watching the ball fall down from the sky. It went through his hands and bounced on the ground. She didn't say anything else and went inside.

"You want me to throw some to you," Exequiel said, "so you can hit?"

"Sure," Wendell said.

Exequiel was surprised.

"Make sure you put some pepper on it," the boy said as he picked up the ball and tossed it to him.

Exequiel caught the ball and stared at it.

"Where do I put this pepper?" he said.

The boy laughed.

"Are you kidding me?" he said. "Really?"

Exequiel smiled. "I *got* you."

"Actually, it's just *gotcha*," the boy said.

"Okay," Exequiel said. "Gotcha."

"See?" the boy said. "Doesn't that just sound right?"

When they fought, Exequiel became silent. He had figured out early that she had been used to men who made a habit of yelling at her and making her feel stupid. Exequiel didn't want to be that kind of person for her. So he listened. When she got frustrated, she said, "Oh, for fuck's sake, would you please just say something?"

It would be as if he had been waiting his entire life to be told to speak. He would try to fill the spaces of silence with every word in this language that he was still learning. He would try not to think about the boy Wendell in the room down the hall, who was probably pressing his ear to the door so he could hear anything, something, and Exequiel knew that whatever he said would be heard by both of them, Wendell and Marsha, and so he tried to say things that could have multiple meanings, multiple lives.

Spaces of silence became the spaces in the boy's smile. The teeth coming in at last had forced others out of their way. He was a good kid. Exequiel felt that even though the father had not been a part of the boy's life—Wendell confessing once to him that he wouldn't know his father if the man fell from the sky and landed on the house—he would grow up to be good person. Already the boy would not speak ill of the man who had abandoned him and his mother. The man who, Elle later explained, had left in the middle of the night—going to the store for cigarettes and bacon, of all things—and never come back.

To her disgust, Joshua still called the house, but only to ask how the boy was doing. Marsha would speak with him. She was pleasant the entire time. Afterward Elle and her mother would argue. The boy knew each time that it was his father calling the house. It was his father who continued to cause trouble.

A recent fight had come about because Exequiel had answered the phone. It was supposed to be a joke. He was trying to make Wendell laugh, especially with the way he spoke into the receiver, disguising his accent and sounding, he thought, like someone from England.

When the voice on the other end asked for Marsha, Exequiel paused.

Elle stood in front of him holding out her hand for the phone. He cupped it and told her the call was for her mother.

"Who is it?" Elle said. "Let me talk to him."

"Hold on," Exequiel said to her.

Wendell watched from the table. He started smirking and stabbing into the mound of macaroni and cheese on his plate.

"Who is it, *do I say,* is calling this house?" Exequiel said. He knew he was making a mess of this attempt.

"Who *is* this?" the voice said.

"Who is *this?*" Exequiel countered.

He didn't like this person's tone.

"Give me the phone," Elle said. She reached for the phone, but Exequiel dodged her grasp. The voice said something that Exequiel couldn't make out.

"I'm sorry," Exequiel said. "What did you say?"

"I said I'm your worst *fucking* nightmare, you *spic* motherfucker," the voice said.

Wendell was laughing now. It was a funny expression on Exequiel's face.

Elle looked at her son. She yelled for him to stop egging him on, as if Exequiel were a child. A boy again.

The voice on the other end only said, "I know you're still there. I can hear you breathing."

Months later, she wouldn't tell him where she got the camera. A gift was all she said it was and played it off until he stopped inquiring. Some nights she had to get away, to get out of her head. She left him at the house with the boy and her mother, who stayed in the back room unless there was a show on that she liked and only then would she come out into the living room to talk with Exequiel, keeping her Bible close, tucked under her arm.

Days when Exequiel could sleep in, he didn't. He would wake before they did and would walk outside and water the plants in the backyard. There were a few Elle kept in large terra-cotta pots.

Inside the kitchen, along the window where he had set aside a coffee can filled with dirt and planted coriander, he plucked fan-shaped leaves of cilantro and ran them under water and patted them dry. There were eggs in the refrigerator and a large overripe tomato on the counter that he would dice and mix along with the fresh herb for an omelet. He had lit the gas burner and was bringing a pan down onto the palm of blue flames when he felt a flash of light against the side of his face.

Elle stood there with the new camera. A small card of papered film started rolling out like a robotic tongue. She grabbed it by the bottom border and shook it out in front of him. She laughed when she looked at it. She said she had never seen a man cook for anyone other than himself.

"You think this is for *you*?" Exequiel joked.

She walked up close to him and set the camera and the picture down together and slipped her hands under his T-shirt and started rubbing him, making sure not to go anywhere near the smooth pits of flesh above his chest and behind the same shoulder. Making sure not to insinuate, with her fingertips, that direction in the least.

She had done so once by mistake and heard him gasp, but just barely.

She realized, when she had finally seen his body in the light, that his scars were old and long a part of him in the same way her father's fingers had melted together, fused within her memory.

Exequiel reached for the camera. He asked her if she would smile for him. It was a question she found endearing, that he would put it this way, asking for permission. When she smiled, he hesitated, suddenly surprised. He slowly brought down the camera. There was her body in full view. And happiness that was wholly their own. He would take more pictures of her, of course, but it was this one moment that would never quite fade for him. The way her mouth eventually fell into an evenness. An expression between a kind of joy and regret.

He had kissed her fingertips and tried not to drag his foot as he walked over to the cupboard and took out some plates and spooned portions for the two of them, covering what was left in the pan for the boy and for the grandmother, both of them still asleep.

"I heard some guys at the store the other day," she said between bites. "They were talking about an opening at the phone company. That's rare, you know."

"Doing what?" Exequiel said.

"Putting up cables, I think."

"Cables?"

"The long phone lines."

"Oh."

He still looked confused.

"Haven't you ever seen guys do that? Hanging up there on poles?" she said.

"I don't know."

"It would be something permanent," she said.

He looked at her.

"Most people who get on with the company do pretty well for themselves."

"I don't know about that," Exequiel said.

"I'd think you'd be good at it. You just have to be a good climber, I'm guessing."

He took another bite of his food and then looked at her again, but differently, in a way that made her think that he had never seen her before in his life.

"What?" she said.

"*Permanente.*"

"Yes, permanent."

Wendell came walking into the kitchen. His hair was a mess of tangles. He'd had a fitful night of dreaming. He yawned and peered at the two of them staring back.

"I could use some coffee," the boy said.

He laughed at his own joke.

"I'm sure you could," Elle said looking away from her son. "You could use a lot of things."

Before he could be made permanent, Exequiel had to prove himself on the job. There was other paperwork to clear, but first things first, they told him. They enrolled him in a class for pole climbing. They called it *working aloft*.

He didn't think he would be able to do such a thing, but it turned out, so long as he took his time and was careful, his body would respond. It would allow him to ascend with each controlled step.

They trained him to use an extension ladder. The swiveled hooks on the top end held what was called the fly section of the ladder in place, along a strand of coiled metal wire. On either side of this strand were telephone poles. The training yard was filled with patches of mulch for cushion in case trainees fell. The poles weeping creosote and other carcinogens made the inside of Exequiel's throat burn, but he didn't want to say anything for fear of being ridiculed.

Once, placing the ladder midspan, he climbed as high as the ladder would go. There was nothing in front of him. Above, there were few clouds left, textured with distance. Exequiel tested the strand with the voltage meter, placing the sharp tip against the coiled wire. Then he went on to loop his leather harness belt through the side of the ladder. The strand wavered slightly. His body tensed.

"You're doing fine," his trainer yelled from the ground.

Exequiel exhaled slowly. He slipped the hook onto the metal D ring, there on the other side of the thick belt. Of all things to be in his mind, he was surprised he could hear the boy's voice telling him it was *all right*. That yes, he knew he was afraid, but there was a reason he was doing all of this, and the boy was thankful for it. He understood that Exequiel had traded out one fear for another.

The boy was, he needed Exequiel to know, aware of such sacrifice. Then he drew comparisons to the lessons Exequiel had already taught him. About the pawn and the knight and the bishop and the rook. The queen, the most powerful piece on the chessboard, could move endlessly in any direction, while the king, of course, was the vital piece that limped along one space at a time. Everything was a sequence that worked toward trapping the king.

To keep him from moving any further.

"Check yourself," the trainer yelled from the ground.

Exequiel had belted in, but the ladder was starting to slide to the left. He leaned forward when he shouldn't have. The ladder slid quickly to the right. His body seized up again. His legs were frozen near one of the top rungs. He suddenly grabbed hold of the strand with both hands and took another breath.

There was nothing in front of him.

That night, he lay in bed and Elle rubbed his legs.

"You can do this," she said. "I know you can do it."

She let go of his left leg and moved slowly up and down on the right one. He tried to breathe through it. He winced, forcing his head to stay on the pillow. Even though he had showered and brushed his teeth, in his mouth was a trace of creosote. He felt as if he had spent the day chewing on the tar-colored glaze.

"They tell me tomorrow we *gaff*," he said.

"What is that?" she said. "What does that mean?"

"Something to do with hooks and braces."

"Hooks?"

She placed her hands firmly on both of his legs. She wanted to keep them from moving.

"They have these metal things they strap to your legs," he said. "I saw a man doing this before we left the yard. He scraped up the pole, sinking the hooks in with each step. I had never seen anyone do that in my life, not really climb like that."

A knock came at the bedroom door. They could hear Wendell's muffled voice asking if he could come in and see what they were doing.

Elle laughed at her son's candor. He went on to admit he was angry Grandmarsha wasn't letting him watch *The Love Boat*.

"Do you mind if we let him in for a little while?" she said.

"Let me put on a shirt," Exequiel said.

Before he could finish getting dressed, Elle opened the door. Exequiel stood there, bare-chested and in his thin boxers. Wendell looked at him with eyes swollen and red.

"What happened to your shoulder?" the boy said.

Exequiel glanced at Elle.

She quickly changed the subject. Exequiel pulled on a new T-shirt and started to leave the room. He could hear Elle telling Wendell it was time he started watching how he spoke to others, especially grown-ups. Exequiel could end up staying for good, and what did he think about that?

She brushed the bangs out of Wendell's eyes. The boy still looked sad. She was whispering to him that if he wanted, he could call Exequiel *Dad*. She thought it might be nice if he did. She asked him what he thought of that.

Down the hall, Exequiel passed the boy's room. There was the chessboard. All of its pieces in place. Between the two sides, a field of empty squares.

The telephone poles had been trees. He tried to imagine them rising out of dirt and bursting, their canopies green and lush. In the training yard, his group studied the class and sizing of each pole.

Elle had told him about her father's stories. Mostly the times the man had parachuted into forests as they burned. Exequiel tried picturing how the trees filled the air with their burning. The smell of smoke cast out for miles on end.

During the middle of the final week, training had ended early, and he was looking forward to getting home and showering. Maybe nap before she finished her shift. One of the guys from the class had dropped him off on the main road, a few blocks from the neighborhood. Exequiel was grateful, though his legs were tired.

Turning onto their street, he was surprised to see Elle's car in the driveway. There was another car there. He didn't know whose it was. It looked new. Maybe Marsha had gone and bought one with some of the money Elle suspected the old woman had squirreled away.

Closer to the house, he slowed his pace. Wendell lay on the ground in the front yard, the bicycle next to him. Exequiel didn't hesitate. He dropped his bag. He yelled Wendell's name.

The boy didn't move.

Exequiel crouched down to check his breathing.

There was no movement.

Then, suddenly, the boy laughed, giggling. He sat up.

Wendell pointed at Exequiel's chest and said, "I got you, Dad."

"You got me," Exequiel said.

"I got you good," Wendell said.

"Yes, you did."

"What's wrong?"

Exequiel finally collapsed on the ground. Beholding the burnt orange sky above them. He let out a breath.

"Are you tired?" Wendell said.

"Yes, that's it."

"Oh."

"Where's your mom?"

"Inside talking."

"With your grandmother?"

"No," the boy said. "With some man."

Wendell picked up his bicycle. "That was a good joke, wasn't it?"

"Yes," Exequiel said. "A good joke."

He remembered his tools and went into the street to gather them. Wendell followed on his bicycle, wobbling as he rode past. Exequiel fought off the urge to say, "Watch out."

The boy went a few houses down and then turned and raced back. Exequiel realized he had never been taught how to ride a bicycle himself. He laughed at the thought that Wendell might one day have to teach him.

"What?" Wendell said as he approached. He hit the brakes and skidded to a stop.

"I can't do what it is you're doing," Exequiel said.

"Do what?" the boy said, smiling. "Ride a bike?"

Exequiel nodded.

"Really?"

"Really."

"Wow."

"I know. You're getting older."

"If you want, I can show you how. It's easy." Wendell studied his face.

"Maybe later," Exequiel said.

He looked at the house. He dragged his foot behind him.

He could hear them in the kitchen. Their silence as he rounded the corner. Elle looked out of breath herself. The rims of both eyes red as flares on a roadside.

Exequiel thought the puffiness of her lips, the faint pink smear on one side in particular, had been from some scuffle, but when he looked at the man standing across from her, the smirk on the man's face, Exequiel knew. On the man's mouth, the same coloring.

Among Exequiel's tools was a thick, fourteen-inch flathead screwdriver that he had been taught that morning to use for testing the integrity of a telephone pole. It functioned more like a dagger. The instructor had shown him how to go around in a circle and stab at the base of the pole, deep into the wood, to see if any of the outer ring would flake off. He had to do this before he started his climb. If he failed to perform this step, he would be penalized.

"This is Joshua," Elle said nervously.

Joshua wiped at his chin and grinned without saying a word.

Even so, Exequiel could still hear the man's voice. He was talking to him on the phone again. Exequiel didn't need for him to speak. He didn't need to be insulted anymore.

He set his bag down and rummaged through the contents until he found the screwdriver. He grabbed at the metal end, holding it to his side like a hammer.

Joshua looked sheepish with his lips smeared pink. Exequiel could not put out of his head that these were the same lips that had formed the words *spic motherfucker*. Exequiel was glad that the voice on the other end of the line could hear him breathing and that now the body that had made the voice had come into his life in this way.

He did not pretend, as Joshua pretended, that everything was fine.

They could not just go back into their lives as if nothing had happened. Everything had already happened.

Outside the boy rode his bicycle.

Exequiel held his breath. His chest shuddered. He thought he could hear the boy racing past the house. The wheels whirring like the engines of a distant airplane. It was headed this way. Inside, the smoke jumpers waited to vanish into an inferno.

The phone number was written on a small slip of paper that had been left inside a book of poems. He found the book in the trunk of the car, under a box of tools. He had kept the same tools over the years, as he traveled from one small town to the next. The motel parking lot was a bleached field of random shoots, cracks spidering out in the pavement. He held the slip of paper and studied the phone number and remembered the boy and the smell of his hair. Elle's way of standing in the kitchen. The warmth of her body as they shared coffee in the mornings before he left for work.

He went inside the motel room and pulled the dusty curtains to the side. Through the window, the sound of the highway threatened to become something else. He wondered if the boy, who had to be fifteen or sixteen by now, would even remember him. He dialed the sequence of numbers. He waited for someone to answer, but no one did.

Later that evening, he ate dinner at the small roadside restaurant near the motel and brought back to his room some coffee and a slice of lemon meringue pie, touted by the lone waitress as a specialty of the place. The pie filling was tart and the coffee was bitter, but he enjoyed them nonetheless. He opened the window and lay back on the bed and listened as the moths gathered on the screen. As far as he knew, he was the only guest.

He tried the numbers again.

This time, a woman answered.

"Who's there?" she said, when he wouldn't speak.

"I'm sorry," he said, struggling. "I must have the wrong number."

"Is that you?" she said.

There was a pause on her end.

He tried to take a breath quietly, so as not to be heard breathing.

"Exequiel?" she said. "Is that you?"

He answered her, and she laughed, saying she thought it was him. She asked where he was. How had he been? Just the other day she was talking on the phone to her brother Wallace. She couldn't remember if he had ever met Exequiel. Then she made a joke about her ex and how his broken jaw remembered Exequiel, for sure. She laughed again. He didn't know what to say exactly, and so he said, "I'm fine. I'm working in Georgia."

"Oh," she said. "I thought you might be closer."

"No," he said.

There were more pauses in the way they spoke to one another. More moths left the darkness to brush the screen.

"How is Wendell?" he said finally.

"Wendell?"

"Yes, Wendell," Exequiel said. "What is it?"

She whispered, but he couldn't make out what she was saying, even when she spoke clearly and started telling him about the boy. He didn't want to hear what he knew she would say, but as she spoke, he could already see the way it had happened. The boy growing up with fresh anger. Having joined with other boys in the neighborhood who shared the same way of looking at the world. Each night they would ride their bikes into the streets, keying cars or throwing bricks through windows. One day, the oldest of them was able to drive and took the boys to meet other boys nearby who were older. She said it had become too much in the house. These boys had begun to hang out at all hours, coming in when they wished.

They had tested Wendell to see what he would do.

At thirteen, he took a bandana and wrapped it around his face like an outlaw and walked into a convenience store and asked the man behind the counter for all of his money. When the man refused, Wendell pulled out a gun. The oldest of the boys had used the gun in similar robberies. Wendell took aim at the man, but the man fell, clutching at his chest. Wendell had not pulled the trigger. It didn't matter.

The paramedics brought the man to the hospital, and he gave a description of the car and the boy who had pointed the gun at him, who had foolishly thrown it down onto the floor and raced off with the others. It wasn't long before the sheriff's deputy came to the house and arrested Wendell.

"I'm sorry," Exequiel said.

He could still hear the boy's laughter, could see him walking slowly into the kitchen those mornings, rubbing his eyes as his hair stood up in back like the broken springs of a clock. Each time, it was the same ritual. The boy would step between Elle and him and pretend he wanted their coffee, just to hear them say, "No, no, you're too young." Then they would hold him.

Exequiel stopped listening to the story. He could hear her breathing on the other end of the line. Somehow they were connected by a thin strand of wire that left the room where he waited to hear her just once more and extended elsewhere, into an unfortunate oblivion.

five

It wasn't long after their time together in Charlottesville that Rachel and Tom were engaged. Rachel had graduated with honors and had job offers from a number of firms in both the Richmond area and a few cities in Hampton Roads, most notably Norfolk. Her aspirations involved going to law school eventually, and she believed experience as a paralegal would help her application.

When they had first met, never in those early discussions about life had she mentioned such an interest. Perhaps he had inadvertently influenced her, describing too often the horror of the crime in his childhood, how his family had been left to make sense of something senseless?

Before the proposal, Tom had been meaning to break things off. The perfect opportunity for such a discussion, though, never seemed to surface. So he waited, but as he did, he grew angry with himself.

One day, he spoke up.

"*Now* you're telling me this shit?" she said.

She threw a glass. It smashed against the wall near him.

Tom clutched his hand. There was blood. He carried the small shard over to the sink. He would not say anything as he ran water over his hand.

Rachel decided to tell him.

He looked up from the running water.

"Yeah, right," he laughed. He thought she was making it up.

"In a month or so we'll hear the heartbeat," she said.

"You're serious."

He turned off the faucet.

His fingers bled slowly into the drain.

"I knew you'd be thrilled," she said.

She wiped at her eyes, but then stared hard.

Tom felt she was looking through him.

"How long have you kept this secret?" he said.

"What does it matter?"

"How long?" he said. It was only now that he felt his fingers throbbing, going numb.

"You're such a fuck," she said.

That night, after they made love, Tom lay awake in bed. Rachel had fallen asleep, was snoring lightly. In the glow from the lamp on the stack of books they used as a nightstand, he read the shadows. They were spread in paragraphs along the warped ceiling. He tried to make sense of what he felt now. "Rachel?" he said, though he knew she was dreaming. He wanted to wake her just then, but instead, he let her sleep.

Teagan had helped her mother clean the kitchen, even getting down on her knees to scrub the floor like Cinderella. She had the picture book in her room. It was one of her favorite things.

"Sissy, get up," her mother said, but Teagan would not relent. She wanted to be the one who was a prisoner. She wanted to clean and then be locked up in a room, and she wanted very much to put on a dress and go to a dance and have people look at her and think she was pretty.

"Tommy needs to see the floor," Teagan said.

"He'll see the floor," her mother said.

"Dad said he wants me to clean it good. Wants to see our faces in the floor."

"He was kidding."

"I see my face."

"Sissy, get up," her mother said, but Teagan refused. She gazed down at her face and kept trying to wipe it away.

After they finished in the kitchen, she helped tidy up the living room and then Elinor started cleaning the main bathroom. Elinor wanted her daughter to take a nap, but there was too much excitement. There was no way Teagan would calm down enough to rest. She had made the mistake of telling her that Tommy and Rachel were coming over later. Manny would be home by then, too. Tommy supposedly had good news to share.

Elinor stood in the shower and sprayed down the tile and let it sit.

"Sissy, what are you doing now?" she called out.

Teagan didn't answer.

"Where are you?" Elinor said.

She heard Teagan laughing quietly, talking.

Elinor went down the hall to Teagan's bedroom.

She found her sitting in the middle of the floor. Teagan's dolls were grouped by size, smallest to biggest, and facing her. They gave Teagan their full attention. She was reading to them. "Isn't this *exciting?*" she said slowly, enunciating the word. She brushed the hair away from each of their faces.

"I'm the teacher, and you better be thankful," she said to the biggest. "You could be locked up for doing that, you know?"

Elinor cupped her mouth and leaned forward in the doorway, but Teagan still hadn't noticed her.

"What was that?" Teagan said to the smallest doll. "What did you say? You don't want to go? Well, that's too bad. Too bad, too bad!" She started repeating the words, even dropping the book to her side so she could use both fists to pound the air.

Elinor saw that Teagan had changed into a dress, but when Elinor looked closer now, she realized it wasn't one of her daughter's dresses, it was one of hers. Taken from the back of the closet, a dress from a long time ago. She wanted to ask her daughter why she had taken it without asking for permission. It had been wrapped up because the pale white cloth was delicate. It was old. Couldn't she see that it was fragile? Why couldn't she?

Tom and Rachel met on Tom's lunch break from the sports equipment store where he had recently found employment. It was the kind of place where his father would love to work. Tom's days were mostly spent replenishing the shelves. If he wasn't helping customers, he was signing off on pallets. New shipments of uniforms. Rows of boxed, untouched soccer balls. Basketball shoes. Boxing gloves. The flow of inventory seemed endless.

Tom might have been consumed by the monotony if he hadn't, only months before, heard the gurgling static of their child's heart. Rachel had tried to keep from laughing. She cupped her mouth. The heartbeat had sounded oceanic to Tom, something immense. It wavered and cradled him. He didn't want to stop hearing it.

Today, they were to meet in a different room. They had been called in because of some questionable test results. An ultrasound had been scheduled and would *rule out concerns*. Rachel had repeated these words more than once, even that very morning. Now, preparing for the technician's arrival, she said them again under her breath. Tom could only stare at her.

Rachel laughed when the technician squirted a thick, warm dollop onto her stretched belly.

"Look familiar?" she said to Tom, trying to get him to laugh.

"Stop," he said. He nudged her.

Had she forgotten about Teagan? Things could still go wrong.

On the screen, a smear of pixels revealed the shape of their child. He quickly tried to discern the image. He looked at the technician's face, her small nose and smaller eyes. There were no signs of change in her expression. He studied the screen and listened as the woman told them everything looked good. She counted out the eyes and measured the distance between them with the computer program. She counted out the fingers and the toes for them. He could listen to this lesson all day long, counting and counting. In the middle of the screen, the heart announced itself in quick bursts of steady flashing.

"I couldn't remember, did you want to know?" the technician said to Rachel.

"Know what?" Tom said.

"The sex," Rachel said to him.

"What about the other thing?" he said.

"It's fine," the technician said, smiling. "Nothing out of the ordinary." Rachel leaned her head against his neck. He exhaled.

"So, do you want to know what you two are having?" the woman said.

six

When Exequiel was a boy, he lay not in the *woods,* for the surrounding area near his town was not referred to as such, but in the realm of trees nearest the ravine that he and his friends called *el más allá.* The beyond.

Where the others had run off to that day, he didn't know. His older brother Paul was gone by then. Exequiel had been left to fill his days with his own wanderings, breaking sticks or batting away rocks, anything remotely spherical, launching it all into the flora.

His boredom exhausted him.

When he approached the river, he found a matted spot that allowed him both to lie down and rest and to still listen to the water rushing below. It moved like the blood inside his body, he imagined.

His life, no matter where he was to go, would always be tied to here, this juncture. From far off came the scent of rain. Maybe a light shower, but nothing like a storm to fear. He closed his eyes. He waited for his future to come for him on its own.

The oldest of the men who had taken him looked to be his father's age. They were ancient. At nine years old, he was not the best judge of age. He was certain only that there were five of them. All were dressed in a similar way. Their uniforms were evidence of their poverty. Soiled khaki pants and old shirts with prominent logos of American companies. If they wanted to, they could easily drop their weapons and return to their towns, disappearing into lean-tos or other such dwellings.

They had taken him to a spot where they had set up camp. It was near a scattering of things people had dumped and abandoned. This was how they had managed, in the periphery of the jungle, to have in their possession a small card table and even some chairs. This layout seemed extravagant. Otherworldly. The legs of each item refastened and repaired with crude materials.

With only a few chairs, though, some of the men had to stand.

Exequiel's wrists were bound with twine. They had pushed him down onto his back and then set one of the chairs directly over the top of his chest, so that he couldn't move from side to side. The oldest man, looming above Exequiel, bent down and asked him if he had any family. Though he was scared, Exequiel would not answer and thought only of Paul and the times they used to take one of their father's T-shirts and fold and roll it a special way so that it would hold together as a ball. The two boys would kick it around, trying to weave it between each other's legs, his brother Paul sometimes being generous and letting him win.

The oldest of the men, his name was Nestor, yelled at the others to get their guest some water. Nestor thought Exequiel must be thirsty. When the old man Nestor asked him with an earnest expression, his leathery face softening just briefly for the boy, Exequiel shook his head *no,* thinking it had been a trick question, that they were planning to throw him in the river should he respond *yes.* When he saw that they were, in fact, passing around a canteen, Exequiel felt his tongue scrape against the dryness of the roof of his mouth. He wished he had taken this old man up on his offer of water.

The old man Nestor took a long last gulp from the canteen and then leaned close to Exequiel's face. The boy winced from the stench, the old man's mouth reeking of wet bread. He asked the boy the names of every man in town. He wanted to know if the boy knew where weapons were kept.

Most especially guns.

The old man Nestor laughed when he mentioned these words, and his eyes, Exequiel could see, had brightened with mischief at the use of this word *guns.* As if the old man Nestor had become a boy again, briefly, and was conspiring to do something he knew he shouldn't.

The others wanted to keep moving north along the river. As they openly discussed their plans, the old man Nestor shouted at them from where he sat. He was angered by their stupidity. He quickly chided them all for revealing any information in the presence of this boy.

"So should we wait here for you to come back?" the old man Nestor said to Exequiel. Exequiel writhed underneath the chair. His shoulders were beginning to burn from being held so long in one place. His legs, they had fallen asleep and it felt to him as if they had been thrust into a mound of ants, and the ants were no longer marching but had, instead, chosen to make a home in his skin. So had commenced the dutiful work of burrowing.

"Guns," the old man Nestor said again, smiling.

He told the boy that if he were released, he must go back and tell no one that they were there. And further, the boy must go to the houses where he knew the guns were and bring them back. Or else the men who stared down at him now would stare down at the ones whom the boy loved, as the boy would be staring down at them all from heaven above.

"**D**o you understand?" the old man Nestor said.

Exequiel nodded.

"And what happens if you don't find any guns?" the old man Nestor said, all teeth.

"I come back and tell you so."

"That's right. And then?"

"And then you leave here."

"Good," the old man Nestor said.

He looked at the others, who nodded, pleased.

The boy was untied and left to recover on the edge of the encampment. He wanted to run, but his legs would not allow it. Then, as if by magic, the movement of his blood resumed and he stood, wobbly at first like a newborn colt, and took off running.

Where were his idiotic friends, he wondered.

They must be hiding. They must have seen at least one of the men. He ran, moving wet leaves out of his way. The humid air lay so thickly in front of him that he felt as though he were running under a damp sheet, one his mother might have hung from a line to dry. When he reached the river itself, he dove in and was immediately pulled downstream by the fast-moving current.

Brownish water seeped in and out of him as he struggled. Paul had forgotten to teach him how to swim the right way, and now his brother was gone.

But then, just barely, he swam.

He was saved by the bend of land that snagged against his body. He was whipped against the land by his body's trajectory through the current. He nearly vaulted out of the water. He quickly landed on the embankment, where his hands slipped into the mud, along with his knees and his bare feet. Before he could steady himself, he fell face-first into it. He coughed the rest of the river out of his body.

A stray dog with a brindled coat was the first to greet him. It limped over to Exequiel and sniffed the dried mud on the boy's legs. Exequiel crouched down. He let the dog sniff his hands as well. The dog scooted back for a moment.

Its tail, thin as a foil, began to swipe the air back and forth.

Then the rest of its body was set in motion. Hysterical, the dog bounced up and down as the boy stood now and started for town. Mud cracked in places and fell with each step he took.

But much of the mud remained as Exequiel neared a group of boys crouched in a circle. They were playing a game using bottle caps. They were flipping them against insects from whose bodies they had already pulled off a wing or two.

The youngest boy, wearing only a long T-shirt, stood up and screamed when he saw Exequiel. The others looked up. They laughed at their friend.

"You fell into shit," one said.

Exequiel only nodded.

They asked him what happened, and he told them about the place where he had fallen asleep and how he had awoken in the river.

"You must have really been dreaming," one said.

"This was not a dream," Exequiel said, holding his arms out wide. He tried his hardest to describe the way the land had saved him, as if it had reached out with a hand and pulled him to the shore. He mimicked the action. The entire time he spoke, the youngest boy stood next to him and scraped at the shapes of mud still clinging to Exequiel's legs.

He let them have their laugh again. Their happiness rushed forward after Exequiel finished talking. It was happiness brought on by a fear that they had almost lost their friend unknowingly. They were grateful he had come back and given them this story.

Even the youngest had stopped giving his attention to the flaking of mud and began to look around at the others and giggle as the boys, the older ones, laughed hard and slapped each other just as hard on the shoulder. Most trailed off, then.

Exequiel was left with Vin, the one in the group whom he had hoped to talk with alone. Vin, a few years older than Exequiel, was smaller, thinner in frame, but his eyes, sunken in their sockets, gave him the appearance of being even older, almost elderly. Each of the boys considered Vin the wisest of their lot.

Vin, in some ways, was like the old man Nestor. The others in the group had only laughed after Vin had started to. It was natural that Exequiel would report the truth of the encounter to Vin. Natural, too, that Vin would see through Exequiel's initial story and wait for the others to leave, as he had, and then ask his mud-covered friend to tell him what, exactly, had happened in *the beyond*.

Exequiel wanted to cry at first, but he knew that Vin would punch him for his weakness. Vin put his arm around his friend's smooth shoulder and walked him behind the nearest house. After the two peered around the corners for good measure and went back to crouching in an intimate huddle, Exequiel found he could speak as he had wanted to all along.

He told Vin about the old man Nestor and the men who were setting up camp not too far from the town. How above all else, it was up to Exequiel to find some guns—one would do—and bring them to the old man Nestor so he could tell the others they were free to move north along the river and into someone else's life.

Vin listened and nodded in spots.

Exequiel was grateful to see his friend agree, though he didn't know exactly what Vin was agreeing to. When Exequiel finished, he glimpsed his friend's sunken eyes, their ruefulness.

"You know you can't give them anything, right?" Vin said.

"I have to. They said so."

"I see. And if they asked for you to suck their dicks, you would do that?"

Exequiel didn't answer.

"Did you?" Vin said.

"Fuck no," Exequiel said.

Vin nodded.

"Here's what we'll do," he said. The boy went on to explain how his grandfather had a pistol that had been broken years ago, long before Vin had been born, in fact. He knew where his grandfather kept the gun. It was in a tin box under the old man's bed.

"I can't give them that," Exequiel said.

"You have to. They'll go away, right?"

Exequiel considered the plan.

"Come with me then," he said to Vin.

Vin shook his head. "I'll get the pistol from my grandfather, but I'm not going with you. They told you not to tell anyone. It's better this way."

Exequiel looked at his friend, who immediately looked away.

"You're scared," Exequiel said.

"I'm not scared," Vin said.

"You are."

"You're stupid."

"At least I'm brave," Exequiel said.

"You're not brave," Vin said.

It was almost dark when Vin made it back to Exequiel. Without any ceremony the pistol was handed off from the one boy to the next. Exequiel took the gun and sprinted for the same spot near the river where he had fallen asleep. It seemed like years ago. The mud was mostly gone from him. Only his hair still bore remnants of the dried mess.

He plunged headfirst again. This time it was the draping leaves and tangle. He regretted not asking Vin to bring him a flashlight, if his family even had one, and he regretted not going to his house to tell his mother he and Vin would be playing longer together this evening. So that she would not worry.

But all such regrets were pointless.

How would he cross the water in the dark?

How would he find them once he made it to the other side?

He had not considered these details. He wondered if perhaps they had not considered them either, and that after some deliberation throughout the day, the old man Nestor had thought better of his proposition to the boy and had told the other men to gather their things and begin their trek sooner rather than later.

Exequiel wished for this outcome.

He wished for it in the same way he wished for his brother Paul to be safe, wherever he was. He wished for it in the same way he wished to leave this place for good one day and go find his brother. Instead of using their father's T-shirt, they would have more money than they knew what to do with. The first thing he was certain they would do would be to visit a place that sold real balls, all leather and perfectly stitched.

Rows and rows of them.

The pistol began to grow heavy in his hand.

He switched it from left to right to left, to distribute the burden of it, but then it was too much. He used both hands. Still, it was too heavy. He stopped running and set the gun down. He stood up for a moment to catch his breath.

It was growing dark where he stood. He walked slowly in a circle. More than nine times around, his age counted out this way. He kept thinking it would be important if he did so. He paused and decided he could do this. He would do this.

He crouched down to pick up the pistol, but now he couldn't find it.

He placed his hands flat on the ground and felt around in the space beneath him. He widened the perimeter in nervous increments. He could hear himself wheezing. He knew if Vin were here, the older boy would slap the top of his head and tell him to calm down.

As Exequiel scoured the dark, he started to think that this, perhaps, was good luck. The pistol would only signal to the old man Nestor and the others that he had found a stockpile, that he was holding out on them.

Yes, he thought.

After more fruitless rummaging, he had convinced himself. He would go to them empty-handed. They would see he was telling the truth. There was nothing of worth in the town that the boy could find.

He could hear the water. He approached it slowly, knowing there were plenty of places he might plunge down. It was so dark. In some parts he had to feel his way with his feet, his arms outstretched.

Before he could make out the light on the river, a match flared at his right. He turned to see the old man Nestor's face glow before the flame extinguished. The first plume of the cigarette's smoke was a white blue.

"The others did not think you would return, but I knew you were smart. I told them so," the old man Nestor said.

"I couldn't find any guns," Exequiel said.

The old man Nestor did not say anything.

"I tried to find some. I did," the boy said.

"Yes," the old man Nestor said.

"I thought there was one, but I was wrong."

"I'm sorry."

Exequiel didn't understand why the man was apologizing.

"I have to go now," the boy said.

"Yes, you do."

"Okay," the boy said and turned, but he felt a hand immediately clamp down on his shoulder.

"How many places did you look?" the old man Nestor said.

"Just that one," the boy said.

"A long time away for just one place of searching."

The boy did not know how to answer.

The old man Nestor laughed.

"You see, it is an altogether difficult place we have found ourselves in, my young friend. I'm not sure I believe you just yet."

Exequiel thought he could hear Vin calling for him. He thought it was Vin who was saying, "Did you find him?" Exequiel thought of running, but he had already played the scenario out in his mind. It ended with his mother under the old man Nestor's chair.

"You can scream. It's okay if you want to scream."

The old man Nestor had finished another cigarette and was blowing the smoke to the side before he leaned over and regarded the boy. They had gagged him this time, and Exequiel thought at least they would not have the pleasure of hearing him scream. This thought had a short life, like a lit match. A stupid thought. He twisted in place. The twine on his wrists burned over the wounds from earlier.

The old man Nestor removed the piece of shirt that had been knotted and used to gag the boy. "Do you want to tell us anything?" the old man Nestor said.

"Yes," the boy said. "Go to hell."

This made the other men laugh loudly. They slapped each other on the shoulders. There was a lantern with a flame drawn down so low that it had been nearly snuffed out.

"I like this one," the old man Nestor said. "I like this one a lot. If only I had more of them at my disposal!" He coughed, clearing his throat. He laughed the deepest laugh the boy had heard among these men.

"I will ask you again," the old man said. "Because I like you."

He stood up with some difficulty and then repositioned the chair, so that one of the front legs, its gnarled end, rested just above the boy's right shoulder. The metal was so cold from the damp earth that, when it first touched Exequiel, he laughed amidst the terror of the moment. It was too much to consider.

It was not a dream, though it felt like one. A beautiful piece of memory that could make him cry. Exequiel woke now, feverish. Out of his head. He summoned it, from the faint scar woven in the bottom of his foot. A story hidden in the flesh.

Maybe it had slipped through the long-ago knit vessels, skin's sheathing, and was whispering him awake, as Paul would have done and had done that one morning he was supposed to be gone. Exequiel had cried himself to sleep during the night, and Paul had stayed, grabbing him now by both shoulders and asking, almost idiotically, if he was awake—*Are you? Are you awake?* In truth, Exequiel had come to a handful of seconds before and had the presence of mind to pretend, for just a little longer, that he was indeed asleep, settled comfortably in a dream. What better thing than to have his brother stay?

"*Mano*," Paul whispered. He held up one of their father's T-shirts and rolled and folded it, as Exequiel had also been taught, and now the stale scent of their father's sweat came between them and hung in the sweltering air.

"I thought you were gone," Exequiel said, rubbing his eyes.

"I was," Paul said. "I came back."

"So that I could beat you one more time?"

Paul laughed.

"Mano, that will be the day."

"That will be the day," Exequiel echoed.

"Come on, let's not wake up Mama. I'll meet you outside."

Paul took the ball and, with it, their father's scent vanished from the small room.

W as it first light that had stepped its way effortlessly through the vacant street, the shimmering choreography of broken glass and gravel? Exequiel watched as Paul negotiated the sliver of field, juggling the cloth ball in and out of a group of shadowy opponents, ghosts of former games.

Then came his brother's taunts. It was expected.

"Mano, you still asleep? Maybe you want I should get Tia and see if she can join in? Maybe you want to play her instead of me?"

The ball rested on his knee. Then it flew up, spiralling, to perch behind his brother's neck. The body hunched before him. The ball like a burden to carry for a long time.

Though he wore no shoes, not even the crudely constructed sandals some of his friends possessed, Exequiel sprinted forward to challenge his brother. He shoved him, knocking the ball free. Paul immediately laughed. He was pleased to see the lesson of aggression had been passed down.

Then another scuffle.

Something inside had possessed the younger brother. Welled up like a curse. Settled in his mouth and split his tongue, a fury. A fire stoked. His tongue burned with words he had never said before, but which he knew were reserved for only the most uncontrollable moments of anger.

Exequiel was mad at his brother. He didn't know why. Then he did. Paul was leaving. It reminded him that he, Exequiel, had nowhere he could go.

Exequiel did not soften his words as he pushed on his brother, flailing with elbows. Fighting for the ball between them. Their father lost within the cloth.

"Let go," Paul said, suddenly serious.

His smile had faded.

"You let go," Exequiel said.

He continued to charge forward, wrapped up as he was in his brother's arms. He wanted to hurry up and be free. He didn't care for other things in this life, like his brother did. Other things were dreams. He wanted what was here, what was real.

Paul complaining plenty of times about the way things were. Paul wanting to go elsewhere, beyond the only place he and Exequiel had ever known together. Northward. Where land shifted out of itself and into other forms. Dreams filled with concrete.

"Mama, I will send money. I will build a huge house and bring you and Mano there to live."

How many times had Exequiel heard this plea? It felt like a plea, to hear his brother repeat it like vespers. And with the same capacity their mother released such prayers in the town's chapel. Too many to name, but always these repeated lines. A prayer ending with a miniscule flame being lit and that flame's life watched briefly, until it disappeared within itself.

Exequiel had, at first, been excited to hear his brother say he would send him back a stitched-leather ball. The echoing remnants of this promise burned inside the boy's desire to overcome his brother. Exequiel wanted to show him he would not back down.

Paul stood still.

"Mano, you need to calm down."

"*You* need to calm down," Exequiel said.

He had resorted to throwing full-on punches. Stepping into each one. Paul just stood there. He wouldn't bring up his guard.

Whatever lingering guilt Paul felt accounted for more than he realized. He had not known what had kept him from leaving the night before. But now he knew. His little brother was making sure of it.

Exequiel had forgotten about the ball entirely, but when he pushed back on his brother, their legs tangled. The cloth ball had found its way between them again. As if trying to break the two brothers up.

Then Exequiel screamed.

Paul knew he had not hit him, but still, he threw his hands up. Exequiel immediately reached for the ground and hobbled over to the side of the empty street. He grabbed his ankle and fell into the grass. Glass, slender as a finishing nail, had lodged in the boy's foot. He waited for the blood, but it did not appear.

"It hurts," he said to Paul, and without saying a word, his brother took the lifted leg and searched for a wound that he could not readily see.

There, in the callous padding of his younger brother's heel, Paul found where the glass had entered. If it were a compass needle, it would have been pointing north. Paul lightly brushed away more of the dirt and could see that it was, in fact, a substantial piece of glass. He pushed on it, expecting Exequiel to scream again, but to his surprise, his younger brother just looked at him.

"You don't feel that?" Paul said.

"I do."

"It doesn't hurt?"

"It does."

"I don't understand."

"I don't understand it either," Exequiel said.

"It will get infected," Paul said.

Exequiel nodded and stood up, keeping his weight off his injured foot. Paul wanted to carry him back home, but Exequiel only leaned against him. He hopped back, wincing as he did, but he made no noise. He would not let on that it was painful.

The two did not wake up their mother. Paul found a pair of bent tweezers that were used for a number of jobs. Since there was no blood on his brother's foot, Paul decided these would suffice and positioned his fingers to push on the spot again, until the glass sliver poked out. With the tweezers, he grabbed the end of the glass and pulled slowly, intent on keeping this most fragile piece intact. But Paul's hands started to shake before the sliver could be removed all the way. The last fragment would have to be dug out. This digging is what brought forth the blood.

Finally, Exequiel prayed aloud.

Later, the echo of such shaking, the nervousness, would remind Exequiel of his brother's inability to be who it was Exequiel desperately needed. Their father, they had somehow taken his memory and hidden it inside a game. Now Paul was leaving, and with him went the endless memories they had fought over.

When the ache rang forth again, it was in the bones of the ankle above the same foot, the very one newly shattered by the old man Nestor's boots. He had kicked at Exequiel as if the boy were trying to keep the ball away from him. And how could Exequiel explain why, despite his mind going blank, he felt a small amount of gratitude for the bitter release?

When Exequiel woke, he felt nothing this time.

Part of the darkness lay in his throat. His head suddenly jolted back. The gag had been removed. There was a strange feeling now, though, as the entirety of the moment came back—like a bucket being lifted, smacking against the stones of a well, and the cold water spilling out and glazing the walls, some of the water falling but the majority continuing on upward, rope tightening in its weave, the excess water in the fibers wringing out as the bucket emerges into the feckless light of day—he screamed inside his head.

This is what saved him.

He had not uttered so much as one whimper. He had wanted to do more than that. He wanted to unhinge his jaw so that he could dump out the contents of his pain. So that the pain would pour forth unyieldingly.

The leg of the chair had long been removed from inside his shoulder, where it had pushed all the way through and endlessly twisted as if searching inside him for some truth. This gesture repeated until he had passed out. Now the wound was a mouth taking in air for him, as the scream continued in his head.

His wrists were still bound with twine, but one of the men had forgotten to secure his body. Exequiel sat up. He could see the bulky shadows of the men as they slept on their sides. They were little mountains of ash and smolder, mudslides all of them.

Exequiel turned onto his stomach. He nearly passed out from the bright light of his wounds, but he inched up, trying to stand. He immediately fell. His foot had been damaged, but the pain was only another version of light as his mind was gripped by only one thought now: a path.

The men continued on in their dreaming.

· · · ·

How far had he gone before he felt he could go no further?

His breathing betrayed him. It was not easily stifled, especially as he had to drag his newly broken foot behind him. Each jut in the path sent a bolt through him. It caused his chest to shudder in the one place that most needed to be kept still. The bolts exited his body over and again from this one wound.

He fell.

He stood up and tried to go on, but could not.

When he fell again, he wasn't sure if he had fallen. He thought perhaps he had reached the river and that the ground had given up, as he had given up. The pain he had felt after waking, the immensity of it, had transformed within him. It was teasing him. He lay on the ground that could have been the surface of the river and floated.

Are you awake? What are you doing, Mano?

He thought he heard his brother Paul calling for him from the other side of the river. The same words came to him. He raised his head slightly, though it was through a great amount of pain that he raised himself up on his elbows and tried to look. Was it the light now filling the edges of the distant trees that made him think, just briefly, that his brother had come back to him, and not only that, but also with the gift of something bought and not handmade? Was it a stitched-leather ball that he juggled with his feet, the ball stalling in the air longer than seemed possible?

The ball across the river was held aloft in the new falling light. Then it dropped and rose erratically. He saw that it wasn't a ball at all, just as his brother became a tree bending. The blur of the ball was a butterfly. It landed on his shoulder. The light touch of it nearly made him pass out. Then he did.

That morning Vin and some of the other boys went looking for Exequiel. When they found him, they were so scared that they didn't think about anything other than grabbing their friend's body and dragging him as best they could across a slower-moving section of the river, where they had crossed initially. It hadn't taken long, given that there were more than a handful of them to carry Exequiel back to town.

They found Vin's grandfather, who in an earlier version of his life had been a medical student. The old man, seeing the boy's condition, covered his own mouth as if to hold the breath inside just a little longer. He remembered why he had given up his dream of becoming a doctor. Though his own parents had been deceased for longer than this boy had been alive, the old man could not shake the feeling that he had not only let his father down by flunking out of university, but he had, in essence, let this boy down as well.

"*Abuelo?*" Vin said.

"Give me a second," his grandfather said.

The other boys were restless. They scooted around and switched positions. Their entire reason for being, up until that very moment, had been to look inward and summon strength they knew they normally didn't possess, and now having done so, they felt entitled by having overcome their limitations. Everyone else needed to rise above his own constraints.

The old man, for one, needed to be doing something, but each time Vin addressed his grandfather, the old man just said, "Give me a second," and the other boys could not understand why the old man was saying something like this. Couldn't he see that seconds were not things that they could touch, that could be doled out?

The deliberations were cut short by Vin's grandmother, who entered the house and dropped the large woven basket she had been carrying.

Fruits rolled onto the floor and dispersed in all directions. She immediately asked Vin's grandfather what had happened. The old man only sat down next to the wounded boy and did not respond.

The other boys paused in their unasked questions.

The old man held his own head in his hands. They felt sorry for this old man, though they didn't know why exactly. Vin explained things quickly to his grandmother, as best he could, and his grandmother ordered the boys to lift their friend off the floor and carry him to her bed.

They were then to gather fresh water. Vin was to start a fire. Why hadn't anyone thought to stop the bleeding, or at the very least, cover the wound from the flies? Some blood had pooled on the floor and left a dark oval. Vin's grandfather did not stir until his wife came back over to where he was punishing himself and asked, "What are you doing?"

Exequiel opened his eyes. Vin yelled for his grandmother.

"Did you hear us talking about you?" the old woman asked Exequiel.

The boy glanced at her but did not speak.

Vin's grandfather walked up beside her. Exequiel's eyes widened.

"What is it?" the old man said. "Did I scare you? I can tell you that it is *you* who gave *us* a fright. I was not prepared to see what it was you wanted to show me. I was not prepared, and now I know I need to think on this. Maybe for the rest of my life I will be thinking about this day."

The old man walked to the other side of the room and sat down in a chair and leaned over. The chair creaked as he gazed at the floor.

"Don't mind him," the old woman said, but Exequiel had stopped listening. He was already thinking about *el más allá* and the butterfly that had found him dying and had flown him back to his life.

seven

February 12, 200–

In regards to: Exequiel X. Guzman
DOC#331VA-77XX

Honorable Members of the Parole Board
Virginia Department of Corrections
P.O. Box 26963
Richmond, VA 23261

Dear Honorable Members of the Parole Board:

My name is Mario Guzman, and for three years, I
have served as a pediatric cardiothoracic surgeon
at the Children's Hospital of the King's Daughters in
Norfolk, Virginia. I am the nephew of Exequiel Guzman
DOC#331VA-77XX, and I am writing to you on his behalf.

It is my hope that after reviewing his record as an
inmate, both his completion of numerous behavioral
health programs, as well as his garnering a GED and
an associate's degree, you will find that he has exhibited
a commitment toward bettering himself as an individ-
ual. In addition, my family and I are willing to provide
him with all the support he will need to succeed.

I know my uncle has expressed deep regret for his
past actions. Or at least, I feel he has. I don't know anymore, actually. Can I be honest with you for a minute?
There is nothing he needs to prove to you. Any of you
people. I'm serious. It's sickening, really, this process.

Your sole expectation seems to be that we build the
case he is no longer a threat to society. That is truly
fucked up. What if he was never a threat to begin

with? What if this all started from a mistake that
bloomed into where we are now?

Would it help to know that I used to wait for her? All
I wanted was a chance to tell her something. I didn't
know what, exactly, but that didn't matter to me then.
I would sit near the far corner of the backyard, on the
other side of their fence, hidden there, and sometimes
they would let her out and I would crouch down and
watch her, waiting. I didn't feel terrible doing so.

Often she gathered small flowers, even dandelions,
and as she did, she would sing to herself a kind of
gibberish. I could never make out the words, if they
were even words. I don't care what anyone says, she
was happy. But a different kind of happy. I saw it for
myself. When I think about happiness now, I think of
those moments of her singing to herself.

I'm sure you're wondering if I ever had the chance to
speak to her. Once, she wandered over to the corner
where I was. It was almost evening. I felt like her
mother was going to call her in at any moment, so I
knew now would have to be my chance.

I stood up.

Maybe I startled her. I think I startled myself more.
I was going to say it, whatever *it* was. The words, I
guess. I swear I was going to say them. But my throat
burned, the words glowing like embers.

I realized I was crying. I was trying to speak but
nothing would come out. She, on the other hand, was
patient with me. Maybe she was confused. She waited

for me to say something. I don't want to say I found this confusion comforting, even though I did. It made it easier that she didn't know. That she would never know.

There, I said it.

I hope you can understand why I'm not sending this to you.

There is no *you.*

Respectfully,

Mario Guzman, M.D.

The neighbor's cat, a gray tabby, had a sizeable piece out of its left ear. It pawed at the glass again. Mario could hear its claws click and then catch on the frame of the sliding door. He knew he should never have started feeding it when he had.

"Shoot him," she said.

He could smell her breath. Ancient and sweet, like figs. Her lips were still colored from the wine. He pushed gently on her chin, trying to close her mouth, and she made a face, as if the touch alone had hurt. She turned onto her side.

"It's a girl, by the way," he said.

She said nothing.

Mario climbed out of bed and stood there, his nakedness held by the dim light. He stretched before reaching for his boxers. For the first time in a long time, he had nothing to do for the day.

"Make coffee," she said.

"I'll think about it," he said.

Just outside his bedroom were the den and the patio door. The Elizabeth River. The cat, wide-eyed, was tapping on the glass. It looked as if it had trapped a fly and was now about to kill it properly.

"I'm not happy with you," he said, sliding the door open. The cat cocked its head. It sniffed at the air like a dog. When the cat entered the house, it did so slowly, almost begrudgingly.

In the kitchen, the cat rubbed its body along the trash can. Back and forth, like a bow across a string, the grating noise almost building into a note.

"I smell it too," he said. He wiped at his eyes.

A plastic container held the remnants of lump crabmeat; the rest of the dried pieces were stuck along the inside of the trash bag. His last girlfriend, Tammy, had been so meticulous. The container would have gone through the dishwasher at least once, and then into the recycling bin.

On a shelf in the refrigerator, Mario found the wrapped plate. The last crab cake. The cat wove in and out between his legs. He pulled off the plastic wrap and set the plate down.

"You want to hear something funny, Queequeg?"

The cat made raspy noises as it chewed. It stared at the floor as if concentrating. The coffee pot was just finishing.

"Who are you talking to?" Janet said.

She wore one of his shirts, buttoned halfway. Her tangled black hair was pulled to one side. She had brought her chunky glasses this time, had smuggled them in her small purse. She looked like a librarian who had just survived a tornado.

"What?" she said. "What is it?"

"Nothing," he said. He reached down to pet the cat. It hissed at him. He didn't move, waiting for the wet sandpaper of its tongue.

She stepped around them both to get to the coffee. "You take cream and sugar, right?" She searched for the container of sugar.

He didn't answer her.

On the side of the refrigerator was a hanging calendar. He saw his uncle's name, a penciled-in X, and the time they had planned to meet written carefully underneath.

She asked him something. Already he could feel himself losing the words. Tammy, at least, had lasted longer. She was prettier, too. She had managed to move in for a while before it had become too much.

"I don't really know much about you, do I?" Mario said.

She looked at him.

"What?" he said.

"I could say the same thing."

"Your favorite book."

"Excuse me?"

"Your favorite movie then?"

"Are you okay?"

"I was just wondering these things," he said.

She stirred her coffee, then slowly slipped the tip of the spoon in her mouth. She looked at him, wanting him to notice, and closed her eyes. He felt idiotic.

"*Manhattan.*"

"I don't believe you," Mario said. He was serious. "You must have dated a guy in college who made you watch that film. Am I right?"

"Why are you talking to me like this?"

"But am I right?"

She ran the spoon under water and placed it into the empty sink. She took a sip and studied his face. She smiled.

"Then tell me your favorite part," he insisted.

"Are you serious?"

"See, I told you. Admit it. There's no way that's your favorite movie." He was pleased with himself.

"Maybe it's at the end when Isaac, the Woody Allen character, realizes he made a mistake breaking up with the girl. He suddenly leaves his apartment. He's decided to go see her, to win her back, but there are no cabs in sight. Nothing for him to take. He's desperate, just starts running down the sidewalk. The camera follows alongside him. But he can't keep up the pace. Eventually, he starts walking, trying to catch his breath. The camera slows down for him. It's funny."

"I don't remember that ever happening," Mario said.

"It did," she said. "Then he starts off running again."

He didn't tell her then that he suspected the cat's real owner wasn't coming back. He had not seen his neighbor for some time; he thought perhaps the man, who looked to be around his own age, had been called up for deployment.

He had met the guy only once, at the end of West Freemason Street. Mario had just finished a run. He was cooling down, walking slowly as he passed the marina. His neighbor had laughed to get his attention. He pointed across the slip to the weathered NOAA building made mostly of cinder blocks. A chalky white research ship was docked alongside it.

"So do you think I have a pretty tough commute?" his neighbor said, gesturing with his fingers. They were tiny legs walking on the air.

Mario could only nod. He wanted to get away from this guy. On the way back to the townhouse, he had heard his neighbor shout, "Queequeg! Queequeg!" Then the gray tabby came running.

Mario waited at the end of the dock now. The structure floated on the mirrored water. He stood there in his running shoes and shorts. He was wearing one of his old Eastern Virginia Medical School T-shirts. He had dressed to put in some miles this morning but had yet to start.

He suddenly wondered what Janet was doing, if she had decided to take a shower. He hoped she had simply gone ahead and left for her own place. The last thing he wanted was to go back and find her still there.

Sailboats began to knock against the pilings. Their halyards rattled incessantly. The current seemed equally stubborn. It rocked the floating dock at intervals. In the absence of sails, masts held sheets of emptiness.

Often, he wondered what it would be like to sail one of these boats. To have a destination and yet not have one. He remembered the story of his grandfather, whose name Mario had been given.

"What happened to him?" Mario had asked when he was younger. "Lost at sea," his father answered.

Instead of beginning his run, Mario found he was held in place, inert. The water, he realized, continued to move underneath him. He studied the rigging of the boats. Each worn tether. Lines swayed into more rattling.

There was one boat, in particular.

A tiny curtain pulled back. He could see there was someone aboard. The person peered at him. He looked away. When he glanced back, the face was gone.

"*Hello?*" It was an older woman's voice. She stepped out of the cabin and walked over near the stern. Though there was a warm breeze, she looked dressed for colder weather. She wore a light lavender sweater, the color of oil on water. White capri pants. A bob of silver hair splashed about her face.

Queequeg came up behind him and began to weave between his legs.

"She's marking you," the woman said. "They do that, you know."

"I'm sorry?"

"Her," the woman said, pointing. "It means you're hers. You'll always be tied to her. She's making sure of it."

The woman called Queequeg with a series of clicks and baby talk. "Is this all right?" the woman said.

Her name was Natalie Purcell. She had been born in Annapolis and grown up in a town embedded among the numerous hamlets of eastern Maryland. She and Clay, her husband of nearly forty years, had a friend who had invited them to Norfolk.

Natalie was going to be a grandmother, she added, adjusting the stylish sunglasses atop her head. Mario didn't ask if Clay would be joining them, nor did he tell her that he wasn't exactly hungry, that he rarely ate, mornings. Queequeg went to the door that led to the sleeping quarters. It scratched at the bottom. It collapsed onto its back and kept trying to slip its paws underneath.

"That's darling," Natalie said.

"Is she going to wake your husband?"

He felt strangely responsible for the cat.

"It's fine," she said. "He loves animals. Both of our daughters had cats."

If he concentrated, Mario could make out the sequence with which the boat brushed against the pier. The ropes stretched taut from cleat to cleat.

"Are you still in med school?"

She pointed at the shirt but then leaned down to place a saucer of milk on the floor. The cat sprang up. It pressed its nose into the milk so quickly that it sneezed.

"Don't you worry," the woman said to Queequeg. "There's plenty more where that came from."

Mario could make out the hospital in the distance, his second home. If Janet had gone into work at the children's ward, she would be pushing a cart around. The cart would be filled with coloring books and other art supplies. She was a happy person, an honest person.

"I'm a surgeon at CHKD," he announced to the woman.

"CHKD?"

"Children's Hospital of the King's Daughters."

She nodded.

"Our eldest, Trina, is a doctor."

"Is that right?"

"She went to Hopkins. She's the one having a boy."

"Hopkins is a great school."

"Oh, I think I already mentioned that, didn't I?" She knocked on her head, like she needed a jolt to set things right.

He stared at her for a moment.

"What is it?" she said.

"And your other daughter?"

"My other daughter?"

"You said your daughters had cats."

"I did?" she said. "I'm surprised."

He knew the look she gave him. She could have been a mirror made of water. He could dive within it and drown. Or she could have been made entirely of air, a breath he could have carried with him on a morning run, inhaling and exhaling. Carrying it for years.

"Does she have a name already picked out?" Mario said.

The woman smiled. "She does."

"Would it be bad luck if you told me?"

He ran.

Ahead now were the homes that lined the inlet of The Hague. Textured brick Victorians. The city's old money on display. Those stuck in traffic along the Brambleton Bridge could look over and dream.

His legs felt purposeful. They burned. He knew all he had to do was keep going. The woman had never told him the child's name. He felt lighter for it. He ran past the bronze sculpture in front of the Chrysler Museum. The giant horse suddenly looked real and violent.

He had been proud of himself until he made it back to the apartment. Janet's VW was gone, the patio door left unlocked. The coffee pot was unplugged. There was no note. He sat down at the table and stared out onto the street.

The street ended.

In his bedroom, he found the bed made. The few things she had left in the bathroom were now gone. The counter looked as if it had been wiped clean. In fact, everything had been returned to its former place. As if she had never stepped foot inside.

In a few days, his uncle would be transferred to a halfway house downtown, where he would have to check in and check out, follow a new set of rules. His uncle was a child again.

Mario closed his eyes.

The room grew smaller.

When he opened them, everything felt askew.

The floor was seesawing.

The phone rang.

"I'm sorry," he answered.

It was the wrong number anyway.

Earlier, when Tom had gone to pick up Micah, Rachel mentioned the impending release. Tom had wanted to reproach her for bringing it up, but instead, he took the overnight bag she held out and told Micah to get in the car.

They both watched him run.

"Bring him home safe," she said.

"I always do," he said.

When Tom pulled the Honda into his parents' driveway, his mother and father were both standing at the front door. Micah jumped out of the passenger's side. He was ten years old now and could sit up front without anyone saying a word about it.

The boy greeted his grandmother first, hugging her. With an air of reserve, he held out a hand to his grandfather. Manny took it with a laugh and shook it vigorously, nearly crying, he was so happy to see the boy.

That morning Manny had gone into the attic and rummaged through the storage area. Most of the items he had brought out were toys the kids had played with when they were young. Tom noticed his father was still in his pajamas.

Inside the living room, they walked around piles of toys.

"Look, Dad!" Micah said. He sat down next to a mound of Star Wars figures. Beside them was a box filled with ships and other vehicles.

"Good, good," Manny said without looking.

Tom and his parents continued on into the kitchen.

There were more things piled next to the stove.

Tom studied his mother's face.

"It's because they're letting him out," she offered.

"What do you mean?" Manny said, watching her.

"Nothing," she said.

She looked at Tom.

"I don't want to start anything." She smiled and patted her son on the arm.

Tom sat down beside his father, who was already scribbling into a crossword puzzle. Micah sped into the kitchen, flying an X-wing fighter in one hand and a B-52 bomber in the other.

"Lolo, have you been playing with these?" Micah said.

A slight moaning came from down the hall.

"I'll go check on her," Elinor said. "Come on, Luke Skywalker."

She placed her hand on Micah's back to guide him. He stood straighter, remembering what his father had said about such things. No slouching, no dragging your feet.

Near the stove was a wall of old bread machines and juicers, rusted pots and pans. Cookbooks were used as shims to keep the wall braced and level so that more items could be stacked. In the attic, there was more inventory. He had not managed to bring it all out.

"It's good you're here," Manny said.

"I wanted to see you," Tom said.

"*Kumusta?*"

"*Mabuti.*"

"That's good," Manny said.

"I wanted to see Mom and Sissy, too. Actually, Micah said he wanted to see his Aunt Sissy. He keeps asking about her."

"That's good. That's real good."

The boy came back into the kitchen and took a seat at the table. Elinor did the same. One side of her face was bright red.

"Aunt Sissy hit Grandma," Micah said without looking up.

"She's been just full of herself," Elinor said.

She touched her cheek, then dropped her hand. It fell into her lap.

"They're letting the bastard out tomorrow," his father said to no one.

"I know," Tom said.

"If I could see him, I'd kill him," Manny said.

"I'm sure you would, Dad," Tom said.

Micah got up from his chair. The spaceship and plane flew into the other room.

His father had borrowed their neighbor's rototiller and was in the backyard crouching beside the bulky machinery, studying the network of levers. He was checking to see what went to where and why. Teagan wanted to leave for the back fence. She wanted to show Micah the buttercups and the dandelions.

Tom thought his sister had said she was going to make Micah a *bucket*.

"That's good, Sissy," his mother had added. "Micah, you help your Aunt Sissy make a bouquet."

"*Bouquet*," Teagan corrected and gulped hard, as if swallowing the word's new pronunciation. She gaped at Micah for a moment and then took off in her awkward way.

The boy chased after her.

"He's a gawky kid," Tom said.

"They both are," his mother said. She laughed to herself.

"Rachel thinks I'm too protective," Tom said. "I should have let him start baseball sooner. The other kids throw so hard now."

"He'll be fine," his mother said. "He's taking life at his own pace."

"Have you figured it out yet, Manny?" his mother yelled. His father was still crouched beside the tiller. He twisted nervously at his gray beard. He had taken off his straw hat with its wide brim and frayed ends. It was his beachcomber look. His time in the islands seemed so long ago. He fanned himself with the hat, even though it was not especially hot.

"Manny?" Elinor said.

"I'm fine, I'm fine," he said. "I'm not an idiot, you know."

Tom stared up at the sky.

. . . .

Manny pushed one of the levers and then pushed it back to where it had been. He stood up and put on his hat. He pulled the cord to turn the engine. It sputtered on, and as it did, his hat fell off his head.

The metallic blades looked like claws frozen in place. Manny pushed his weight down on the shuddering handles, but he was having some trouble. The machine finally leaned back. He pulled another lever and the claws began to churn freely above the ground.

He lowered the front so the gouging would begin.

He walked it forward through the vegetable bed, pulling back in spots. When he reached the end of the row, he turned and started a new row.

It was this small progress that made Tom smile. He glanced over at his mother. She had been crying.

"I'm sorry," Elinor said. "This is rare for him."

Tom looked past his father to see how Micah was doing.

"He's all right with her," he said, not realizing it had sounded like a question.

"He's fine," his mother said. "She just doesn't like me lately."

His mother took a minute to get to her feet and peered to where Teagan was bending down and pointing out more flowers for Micah to pull.

"She seems better," Tom said.

His mother glared at him.

"She does," he said, as if to convince himself.

"It's not her, Tommy."

He noticed she was observing his father.

Manny guided the rototiller slowly.

"Look at me," she said. She wiped at her face.

"How long has she been like this, Mom?"

She stopped him. "It was really nothing."

Tom watched his father. Manny turned the rototiller and started going in the opposite direction. He went back over the black rows of soil. The square he was making grew darker.

"Do you ever wonder?" Tom said. He didn't finish his thought.

"All the time," his mother said.

Micah was holding two of the dandelions he had gathered above his head. They dangled like a pair of antennae. Teagan was squealing, running up to him and then away. He was pretending to be an alien. Tom smiled. He remembered he had done the same thing to Micah a few weeks back at a park.

"We found a place that will take her," his mother said finally. "It's really pretty."

. . . .

Micah and Teagan brought over a handful of buttercups.

He knew he had no right to be angry.

"Did you have fun?" Tom asked Micah.

Before the boy could answer, Teagan shouted, "Fun, fun, fun!"

She asked her mother if she would weave the flowers into her hair.

Tom didn't think the flowers would stay and said so.

Elinor smiled and reached into her jacket pocket. She produced long pieces of string, all of equal length. She used the string to weave and hold together a tiny crown of flowers. Teagan blinked as the crown was fastened on her head.

"You look like a princess, Aunt Sissy," Micah said.

"Princess!" Teagan said and clapped.

"That's right," his mother said. "You're *our* princess."

"When I'm old like Tommy, I get to be a woman."

"That's right."

"Then I live in castles and you come visit me," Teagan laughed. "I tell you what to do, and *you* do it, Mama."

Micah laughed.

"That's right," Tom's mother said absently. "I'll come visit you in your castle. Stay steady now, or the flowers are going to fall out."

Teagan froze.

"It's hard, Mama."

"What's that, honey?"

"If I move, I breathe."

"You *silly goose*. You have to breathe," Elinor said.

She stuck her tongue out at her grandson. Micah grinned and ran into the house.

"What's wrong, Mama?" Teagan said and wiped her mother's cheek.

"Nothing's wrong, *silly goose*. I was just thinking. That's all."

"You call me Princess."

"Okay, Princess. I'm sorry. I don't know what in the world I was thinking."

Teagan spread out her arms and walked forward, steadily, as if on a tightrope.

"I fall," she said.

"Don't do that," Elinor said, laughing now.

"I will. I fall."

"Keep your head straight. You're not going to fall."

Tom watched his sister place one foot in front of the other.

He pictured her on a tightrope. High above them. The flowers part of the costume. He wasn't going to say anything. He didn't want to break her concentration.

As they were leaving, Manny told Micah he could take one toy with him, that he had to leave the others for the next time he came to visit. The boy nodded at the bribe.

"They're all yours, Lolo," Micah said with a serious face. "You keep them all."

"All of them," Manny said. He was embarrassed now. "They're your dad's toys. This whole side belongs to him. This other side belongs to your Aunt Sissy."

"Then they should clean it up!" Micah said.

Tom watched his father's smile fall.

The boy took the keys out of Tom's hand and ran for the car.

"You and Mom are coming to his game tomorrow, right?" Tom said. "It's the first one."

"What game?" Manny said.

"Oh, he knows what game," Elinor said. "We'll be there with a bullhorn and a banner."

It was a strange name. Shoe sat on the bench across the street from the halfway house and looked up at the street sign. *Omohundro.* How had such a name made its way to this part of the world? It had to mean something.

Behind him, children at the nearby school were out for recess. He could hear their piercing voices. They traded off chasing one another.

He thought of Mario from years back.

How his nephew had loved to play ball into the evening.

Hadn't he also, as a boy, loved the sound of bodies scuffing the grass of a field? He and Mario were so alike in this way. But then this boy had vanished into another version, one who would endlessly write letters explaining how he was going to make something of his life. Mario had gone on to study hard in school. His nephew was not only a physician, but a surgeon.

A real surgeon, Shoe had bragged to his housemates.

His nephew practiced medicine at the children's hospital downtown.

Shoe could walk there from the Ghent section. But there was no need. Mario was going to pick him up and take him to lunch.

Once he was released altogether, he would go to live with his nephew.

That was the promise.

He sat on the bench and mused on the name of the street again. He closed his eyes. The sounds of the children chasing each other became the sounds of the cars passing in front of him.

Then the idling engine. A vehicle had pulled up close to where he sat.

"Hey, *old man,*" a voice came from inside a silver, pristine Range Rover.

"I got your old man right here," Shoe said and grabbed his crotch.
He climbed inside.

"Where to, Tio?"

Mario was still wearing his scrubs. He was going back after lunch.

"What was it you do again?" Shoe said.

Mario laughed. He knew what his uncle was up to.

Mario announced it with more flair than he normally would have. "I'm a *pediatric cardiothoracic surgeon.*"

"I'm guessing anyone can be one of those," Shoe said.

"That's right," Mario said. "Anyone."

It was warm outside. Shoe welcomed the breeze through the open window. They pulled up to a light. A woman in her mid-forties stopped alongside them. She was driving a faded black BMW. The color made Shoe think of water. A body of water, in particular, one in a poem he had read so often that he had memorized it easily.

In the prison library's possession was a collection by the poet A. R. Ammons. Shoe's favorite was "Corsons Inlet." He liked the way the person inside the poem spoke to him. Of the many lines he loved, in crossing the yard, he would repeat the final line in his head, *That tomorrow a new walk is a new walk.*

"Tio, tell her she looks good in that car," Mario laughed.

Shoe looked at the woman and smiled. He knew she could hear his nephew.

"Your car's beautiful," he finally said to her.

"I'm sorry," she said, turning to face him. "What was that?"

She was wearing designer sunglasses. She had salon-blond hair. She lifted the glasses so that he could see her green eyes.

"Nothing," Shoe said.

The woman replaced her glasses. Her jawline clenched.

The light changed, and the woman drove away.

She had reminded him of someone.

Paul Guzman was happy to see his brother. He could embrace him in his own home. Mary came around the corner, where she was busy cooking a huge meal. She hugged him quickly. Her hair carried the scent of roasted chilis. She was crying.

Shoe didn't know what to do at first. He thought she was going to tell her son to take his uncle back where he had found him. But then he remembered her letters expressing such gratitude. She kissed Shoe on the mouth. Paul had done the same.

Mario's sisters, who had both driven up from Florida, were there with their families. The children, who had been running around in the backyard, were now busy darting into the house, assuming the roles of entitled grandchildren.

"This place is exactly how I remember it," Shoe said.

"We're so glad to have you home, Exequiel," Mary said. "You've brought us good luck, you know that?"

"That's right, Mano," Paul said.

"Yes," Mario said, trying not to cry.

Shoe looked around the room at everyone, then focused on the floor. There was his right foot, turned just slightly askew as if it might walk out the door on its own.

"I just wanted your life," Shoe said quietly, "to be different from mine."

Mario had been the only one to hear his uncle. He found he could barely breathe. The others started clapping, Paul suddenly overcome with the need to vocalize a *grito,* surprising his family as the joyous scream lifted and sank like netting in the wind.

Someone turned on music, something traditional already programmed in the iPod. Paul took Mary's hand. Even though she playfully refused at first. He coaxed her into the widening circle of the room. He held her close. As they spun, he saw his younger brother's face.

"You're a silly man," Mary said to Paul. "It's your brother's turn to dance."

Paul nodded and handed her over to Shoe. Shoe only shook his head. He pointed at the floor, as if the toe of his boot had been nailed into place.

The meal was a number of dishes that Shoe had only been able to dream of for so long—*panes rellenos, yuca frita, pupusa, arroz con chorizo,* more spices than he knew.

Shoe could not eat the meal without being reminded of Mary's skin. The way her neck and hair had smelled when she had embraced him and tried to get him to dance. He did not like to dance. He could not move his body gracefully like the others.

After he finished his meal, his nieces cleared the dishes and brought out a plate of flan from the refrigerator and sat it in the middle of the table. Some of the younger children asked if they could have ice cream instead, and this made Shoe laugh. The other adults laughed too.

Mario looked at his watch and apologized to everyone, especially his uncle. He explained that he needed to get back to the hospital. He took a deep breath. His mother wanted to send him off with a Tupperware container full of food.

"Leave him be, Mariposa," Paul said. "Your son has to go save more lives."

Shoe glanced at his older brother. He could see the pride on his brother's face. He wondered if it was showing on his face as well.

eight

Mario didn't know why he had found it suddenly difficult to breathe. He should have been happy, standing there in his parents' house with his sisters up from Florida, his nieces and nephews having the run of the house. But then there was his uncle, in the middle of it all, among the food and the music and the happiness.

He parked in the reserved space and went inside.

Everyone he passed knew him, knew he was a rising star on the surgical team. He went to conferences all over the country. He never stopped trying to learn about the latest techniques. Even though computers were taking over, a mind was still required to guide the machine.

And then there were instances when all was abandoned for the skill of the surgeon, the steady human hand. He had that. He had cultivated the evenness. Now, though, he was having difficulty breathing. He smiled as he passed nurses and other attendants. He could not shake the way his chest felt. Closing in on itself.

He could label every sheath, every piece of tissue and bone that would converge to make it so. If given the chance, he could open himself up. He knew he could point to what needed to be there, what was essential. Even what needed to be removed.

Opening day began with team pictures. Micah had chosen the number 10. It was his age. It was also the number on the jersey he had found in the closet at his dad's apartment. The jersey wasn't for baseball, but he wouldn't hold that against his father. The cool thing was that it was shimmery and gold. His father had let him wear it to bed that night since he had forgotten to pack his pajamas. Just before his dad had shut off the light, he told Micah a story about a boy who played on a field, who kicked in the winning goal.

"Who was that?" Micah said, laughing.

"You," Tom said. He placed his hand on the boy's chest. "Inside there."

Tom had watched Micah run to catch up with his teammates. The kids were taller, with scowling faces. Some had modified uniforms. Longer pants with belts like the pros. Tom remembered it was Rachel who had insisted they not go all out, since this was just a trial.

"Don't let your guilt buy him an expensive bat," she had said.

"But I can get an employee discount," Tom had said.

"I don't care. There's nothing worse than seeing a kid with everything, all new equipment, get up there and strike out."

He knew she was right. But the impulse to provide for the boy was too great. He had compromised and had bought Micah a batting glove and a mouth guard and wrap-around safety glasses.

Orange and black jerseys bounced up and down. Micah's Orioles uniform looked too big for the boy; the large, freshly screened number 10 covered most of his back. The jersey had been scrunched down into the bunched elastic waistband of his bright white polyester pants. The entire ensemble could have been a construction sign, it was so large and at odds with the boy's frame.

They gathered in the dugout. Tom made sure not to stand near the chain-link section. He would not call Micah over to him. They had worked on his swing earlier.

"Drive it," Tom wanted to tell his son, as if that would mean anything now.

The boys horsed around on the bench. They raked sunflower seeds with their cleats. Wet shells were smeared on the concrete. The boys were laughing.

Tom didn't want to take him away from that.

He climbed the bleachers and took a seat. He saved space for his family. Rachel was going to make the next game. They had already worked out the details, how they would trade off throughout the season.

It was better this way.

The boys went out onto the field and removed their caps.

Tom took off his old UVA baseball hat. One of the fathers had turned around and asked him what year he'd graduated, pointing.

"I didn't," Tom said. "Sorry."

As the prerecorded "Star-Spangled Banner" played out over the brittle speakers of the PA system, Tom glanced back at the parking lot. He could see his mother and father. He searched quickly for Teagan. He was relieved she wasn't with them.

Micah was right in the middle of the lineup, which surprised Tom. He thought for sure his son would have been at the bottom.

"How is he?" Manny said.

"They just started," Tom said. "Where's Sissy?"

Tom's father didn't say anything. Tom leaned over and looked at his mother.

"She wanted to go to one of the craft classes," Elinor said. "That's all."

"What craft class?" Tom said.

The pitcher for the other team, a barrel-chested kid, was throwing hard. He had a gun, but he wasn't very accurate. If anything, it would be a long game. Lots of walks until this boy was traded out.

"It's nothing," Elinor said. "She said she wanted to go to the center, so we dropped her off just to see. We'll get her after the game."

"That's right," Manny said. He was giddy now. He called over to Micah, who was on deck. "Don't swing like a *sissy!*"

He had meant it as a joke, but the boys in the dugout had picked up on it and were chanting, "Sissy! Sissy!" at Micah until their coach, standing near first base, asked them what their problem was.

The bases were loaded when Micah stepped up to the plate. He banged the rubber pentagon. Micah looked over into the bleachers for his dad's approval. Tom gave him a thumbs-up, and Micah laughed.

Before he fixed his stance, a ball flew past his shoulder.

"Strike!" the ump said, turning to the side.

"Come on, *Blue!*" Tom said.

Micah had jumped out of the batter's box.

"Get back in there, son," Manny whispered, his leg bouncing.

Elinor put her hand on her husband to calm him.

The pitcher started his windup.

"*Ball!*" the ump said.

"Good eye!" Tom yelled. It had been the third straight.

A little boy had been milling at the bottom of the bleachers. Someone's younger brother. "*Good 'ay, good 'ay!*" the little boy said. He didn't look up from the small dump truck he was pushing across the gravel. He had sounded Australian.

Manny laughed.

"What's the count?" Elinor said.

"3–1," Manny said. "Come on, Micah. He's all yours now. Get your elbow up!"

Tom felt guilty for having filled the boy's head with too many things.

If you're behind with strikes, work your way back.

Watch for junk.

Only swing on what you can hit.

Micah had stayed in the box through the last three pitches. Now all he had to do was settle in and wait for the next one. It would have to be a strike, or else he'd get walked.

Swing for the fences.

"It's all you, Micah," Tom said.

Micah looked back at him and smiled. He pounded the plate hard and pulled up the new bat, locking the bright barrel into place. There was a slight swagger in his stance. Tom hadn't seen this side of his son. He would have to mention it to Rachel, for sure.

The boy on the mound started his windup again. Tom watched the arm pull back like the hammer on an old-fashioned pistol. Then the wrist unlocked with a jolt as the rest of the body lunged forward. The ball flew into a bullet.

Tom watched it cross the stretch of space. But it was wild and curved.

Micah, instead of hitting the deck, had turned toward it, facing it head-on. It seemed practiced. The boy's arms had simply dropped, pinned back, as if the weight of the bat had been too much. The ball slammed the middle of his chest.

"**N**o!" Tom yelled, jumping off the bleachers.
He had run out onto the field without hesitation.

Micah lay collapsed at the plate. No one had moved. The players and coaches were stunned, the ump frozen.

Tom could not say anything. He didn't care that the ump had come to life and was pleading with him not to move the boy. Tom lifted Micah into his arms. He wasn't going to wait for an ambulance.

"Mom? Dad?" Tom said, confused, bringing the boy to his parents.

"Go," his father said. "Just go! Run to the car!"

"Tommy, go!" his mother screamed.

On the backseat, Micah barely opened his eyes.

"Dad?" he said, crying.

"It's okay," Tom said.

"Dad?"

"You're fine. Do you hear me, baby? You're fine. You're fine."

Tom kept saying these words, "You're fine," as he sped along Hampton Boulevard, toward the downtown. He said it as if to make it so.

The trauma sustained had produced a huge contusion, as if someone had spilled jelly and smeared it under the boy's skin.

At first, upon Micah's arrival to the emergency room, the attending physician suggested only an ice pack and, after checking Micah's vitals, was pleased by the apparent confirmation of his judgment. He found nothing out of the ordinary.

Boys will be boys, the young doctor told Tom and even laughed.

Then Micah fainted.

Mario was sitting by the lockers, in the dark, when he heard the call come over the intercom. His mind switched over, filled now with the light of the screens he knew were waiting for him in another room. The intense graphics swirling with colors, crushed with pixels. He could look into the space of a body and then the representation of it. He searched images for the question.

No, the statement upon which he had built his life.

You must fix everything, Mario.

After prep, he could start to breathe. It was fine. His uncle was free. So was the next breath Mario took. It was getting easier again.

When he saw the last name on the chart, his throat closed. He backed away from the entrance to the operating room and tore off his gloves and then his mask. He did not feel the door at his back, did not realize he had turned and walked into the bright hallway, the artificial light. The floor shiny as ice.

He dodged bodies, ran past those being wheeled away. In the glass wall of the gift shop, pink and blue stuffed animals were stacked in a checkered pattern, a large, plush chessboard turned onto its side.

"Hello, Dr. Guzman," someone said as he darted through the lobby. The automatic doors were not fast enough. He banged on them until they finally slid open.

Under the entrance awning, a young father was nervously securing an infant car seat inside a new minivan. The new mother was pushing herself slowly up out of her wheelchair. She was laughing at her husband, who was laughing as well. He was telling her, "Stop, stop, you're making me mess up."

· · · ·

There, in the sun, Mario paused.

He hunched over, put his hands on his knees, and took a deep breath. A voice inside his head told him to call in Dr. Williams. She could take over. Yes, that made sense. She had more experience. Plus, he knew this family. It might affect his ability to do the best for them.

Some of the cold air from the hospital was still in his clothing. He raised up. His face was warm, his eyes wet. He realized he might cry out at any moment. Across the parking lot, the glaring windshields seemed to blink on and off. Little lights, eyes staring back at him.

There was no time to wonder where the owners of these vehicles were, if they had driven themselves here for a procedure. If they were even still alive. There was no time to think about his place among it all, where he fit in. No time for Janet. No time for Tammy. All he knew was there was a child in the building behind him who would almost certainly die if he didn't turn around and go back.

There was no going back.

He didn't know how much time had passed.

"Dr. Guzman?" one of the nurses said. "Are you all right?"

He looked at her covered face, her skin lit from the screen she stood next to.

Others appeared to him the same way.

He nodded.

When he was a boy, he had loved the feeling of disappearing into a day. He had loved the way he could run with the other boys from the neighborhood and play until the sky grew dark and the world was a cool blanket of air.

The world's one job, it seemed then, was to wrap itself around you, and you tore it off, grappling. It wrapped around you each day, and again, you tore at it and tore at it until one evening the sky was no longer a covering comforting you. It was just an untouchable thing, like so many other things in your life, and the way back, once it became so, was lost. There was no looking back at the path. The path had been swept clean. The earth no different from the empty sky, all of it pressed into one indecipherable puzzle.

Often, he would sit in his room and study while he heard the familiar voices of boys racing past his house. Too many times to count, he would pray that the chains on their bicycles would snap. Not so that there would be an accident, but so that he could find his old friends outside his house, crouched beside the bicycles' pedals. He would imagine himself running into the garage to bring out his father's tools. Wrenches and grease. Pliers too. All of it he would use to find a way to make it right again, so that they could ride off from where he would be standing in the road, a smile on his face, his friends telling the others that he was not bad, that no harm would befall them for treating him as they used to treat him. He was still their friend. He was still a boy.

He had found a tear in one of the arteries.

Some evenings he would sit on the steps of the front porch and watch the others race down the street. They were so fast. He had tried to bring out his bicycle, to race too, but they were gone.

He wondered if that had ever happened. The boys vanished so quickly, they had made it a point to leave him. His part of the street grew quiet. He didn't blame them. How could he blame them?

Whenever he thought he wanted to be part of the games, he would think instead of what was expected of him. The quiet books in his room, the endless words that waited to live inside his head.

That was the pact he had made with the sky and the empty streets of his childhood. Each night, the conversation of his adult self whispering to him, telling him that it was all going to be okay, that he was going to make it right, he only had to do something extraordinary, and for the rest of his life. That was it. There would be more emptiness because that was the way it was.

He remembered the feeling of emptiness. A hole in the landscape of who he was.

It was there for him each night he dreamed, there for him when he woke in the night screaming. His mother would come into his room and quiet him, and he would fall asleep hearing her sing, or what he thought was her singing. He didn't know if it was his mother or the girl. Things he learned were meant to fill the days.

A seam had come undone inside the boy. It filled the screen with red. More gauze and siphoning. The red bloomed again. Someone called out a series of numbers. The speaker's voice was even, almost calm, but the numbers suggested the blood pressure was dropping. He studied the screen, using it as a guide.

He could not get the bleeding to stop.

If he could get the bleeding to stop, it would be a start.

He felt padded gauze dab his brow. He realized he was sweating more than was normal for him. He had waited too long. The bleeding would not stop.

He wanted to go back to the moment. He wanted to stand among the machinery of that evening and listen to her squeal with excitement. Instead of taking aim, he would hold back. He would do everything the same as he had, except for one thing: the ball would never leave his hand. He would hold onto it. As long as he held the ball to his chest, he would never have to see the emptiness of his life. He would never have to run away.

Someone suggested they had lost him too many times, that it should be called.

"No!" Mario said. This wasn't a game to call. He knew the boy's parents were in the waiting room. He could feel them on the other side.

"It's for me to say when this is over," Mario said. "Does everyone understand that?"

Teagan had made everyone a gift—tulips of construction paper. She kept asking if she could give Micah the gift she had made for him.

"Then when can I, Tommy?" she said, but Tom did not answer her again.

Rachel had not yet arrived. Tom kept pacing, his face unchanged.

"Did you get her on the phone?" he asked finally.

His mother only nodded.

"Tommy," Teagan said. "You go get Micah right now. You tell him Aunt Sissy said to come here."

"Sit down," Manny said.

"I can't," Tom said.

"I'm not talking to you," his father said. "Sit down, Sissy."

He walked over to Teagan to get her to take a seat in the chair next to them, but Teagan jerked away. When she did, most of the paper flowers tore apart. They fell to the floor. Tiny ovals littered the ground around her.

Teagan made to scream, but no sound came.

It was as if her voice had disappeared from her throat altogether.

Then a deep breath filled the void.

Tom looked at his sister; her face shuddered. It was obvious this one mess had devastated her. It was more than he understood. She threw her head back and wailed. A sound that came from somewhere inside her.

They could only watch.

When he walked into the waiting room, Mario spotted Teagan. She was standing in a corner and hugging herself. There were Mr. and Mrs. Serafino on the couch. They were much older, but he recognized them. Mrs. Serafino had her arm around a woman and was consoling her.

When Teagan saw who it was, she ran over to him.

"Look, Tommy, look," she said.

Mario turned around. Tom regarded him.

He wanted to tell Tom he was sorry.

He wanted to tell Teagan most of all.

But now was not the time. That would come later. He would go to their house and tell them how it had happened, how he wished it had never happened. His entire life, it seemed, was hanging on this apology.

"The boy's fine," Mario said.

"What?" Tom said. "What did you say?"

He started crying.

They both did.

Where had the years hidden within him? He was still young, though not accomplished in a career like Mario. But there was still time, he thought. Time for everything. He could still see Mario's face as he sat on Tom's parents' couch, trying to find the words to explain why he had run away that evening. Why he had let everything unravel as it had. And as for Mario's uncle, there were no words. That was another kind of burden altogether.

Tom's mother had made an appointment with a neurologist. His father was showing signs, worsening. Had been for years, now that Tom really considered it. More heartache ahead, of course, but at least his father was still here. As was Teagan.

He had told his mother not to worry; he would go to the center and get her. When he was signing her out for the day, she told him she wanted to see geese. She wanted to see flowers. Tom immediately thought of the botanical gardens near the airport. One could watch planes take off from a viewing platform. Micah would love it, he was sure. There was a field there, too, where Teagan and his son could play. He could watch them both.

Micah ran up and slapped his arm.

"You're it!"

The boy threw off his windbreaker. Bright as the azaleas in the distance. He grabbed his Aunt Sissy's hand and the two conspired to get away. There was his sister, and there was his son.

He smiled and unfolded his arms. It felt good to breathe. He laughed, watching their playfulness. Rachel would not have recognized him, not that such a thing mattered. People were allowed to change.

His son had just told him he was "it," and his only job now was to chase after him. Micah and Teagan separated. There was Teagan running ahead, getting farther away. Micah held his arms out and started whirring across the fresh-cut grass.

Then came a giant shadow rumbling, the sky breaking apart.

Teagan brought her hands up and covered her ears.

They all three did.

Micah was grinning, catching his breath.

Overhead, people were being carried away from the city. Beyond clouds. Tom thought of the model airplanes he and his father had worked hard to put together. The one Tom loved the most, fastened with clear string to a hook on the ceiling of his childhood room.

How often had it simply spun on its own?

If he thought hard, he could remember the way it was. He could still see the string and then not at all. Though he knew it wasn't gone entirely, woven as it was into a boy's heart.

acknowledgments

Many people have helped me along the way, and I'm grateful for their presence in my life. If you want to know who the best agent in the world is, I'll tell you: it's Terra Chalberg. I'm especially indebted to Daniel Slager for his guidance and enthusiasm. Allison Wigen, Anne Horowitz, and the Milkweed Editions family have been amazing throughout this entire process. Others who've been supportive in the creation of this book include Ben Barnhart, Maurice Browne, Oliver de la Paz, Brian Flanary, Sarah Gambito, Fred Leebron, Joseph Legaspi, John Moore, Nick Montemarano, Alan Michael Parker, and the luminous souls at Elliot's Fairgrounds in Norfolk, where, for countless evenings, I wrote portions of this manuscript. And for my wife, Amy, who waited up for me.

Jon Pineda is the author of the memoir *Sleep in Me,* a Barnes & Noble Discover Great New Writers selection and a *Library Journal* "Best Books of 2010" selection. He is also the author of the poetry collections *The Translator's Diary,* winner of the 2007 Green Rose Prize from New Issues Poetry & Prose, and *Birthmark,* winner of the 2003 Crab Orchard Award Series in Poetry Open Competition. He teaches in the low-residency MFA program at Queens University of Charlotte and lives in Virginia with his family.

Interior design by Connie Kuhnz
Typeset in Minion Pro
by BookMobile Design and Publishing Services